The Tower of Blue

Eric Locsh

D1202602

For anyone who has struggled to find their voice

Eric Locsh
The Tower of Blue
© 2018, Eric Locsh
info@thetowerofblue.com

All rights reserved.

This is a work of fiction. Names, characters, businesses, places, events, locales, and incidents are either the products of the author's imagination or used in a fictitious manner. Any resemblance to actual persons, living or dead, or actual events is purely coincidental.

Acknowledgements

To my mom and dad, who gave me everything so I could follow my dreams; to my editors, Kaitlin Severini and Mary Auxier, for elevating my work beyond anything I imagined it could become; to my cover artist, Nooch Jung, for making the Tower come to life; to Kelvin Rivera, for pulling the writer inside me out into the light; to my former and current colleagues for reading inferior versions of my manuscript for free, yet still encouraging me to keep writing; and to anyone who has ever taken a chance on me, none of this would be possible without you.

1

MAKING WAVES

In front of a dark home, a midnight dew began to freeze over the freshly cut lawn. A middle-aged man in tight white underwear tiptoed across the grass, looking over his shoulders. Just a few hours earlier a robber had fled the neighborhood. That a robbery would ever occur in his quiet, suburban neighborhood, the man thought, was mad.

The man scurried up the porch steps, his bare feet leaving wet prints on the concrete. He tapped his foot nervously and then knocked on the door in a quick succession of three. His erratic breath hovered around him in the cold air as he hugged his broad figure for warmth.

He knocked again.

A light from the window on the second floor flicked on and the man looked up. He rubbed his palms together and blew forcefully into his hands, repeatedly stepping from side to side. Footsteps approached the door, and he heard the peephole cover sliding open. The man quickly ran his thumb through the waistband of his underwear, smoothing it out, keeping it firmly underneath his gut.

"Mistah Brue?" a man's voice called from the other side of the door. He had a Chinese accent.

"It's *Blue*," the man answered. "And yes, it's me. I'm sorry to wake you, Mr. Wu. Can you open the door? It's freezing out here."

A chain lock rustled from inside and the door crept open. Mr. Blue shoved his foot through the opening and barged into the Wus' foyer. He was hit with an overwhelmingly pungent smell of raw garlic and mothballs.

"I have to use your phone," Mr. Blue demanded, marching into the kitchen.

Mr. Wu chased after him. He was tall and thin, with long arms and a bowl cut of thick black hair and eyes that were too big for their sockets.

"You are naked in my home," Mr. Wu proclaimed, looking Mr. Blue up and down. "What are you doing?"

"I'm calling the cops," Mr. Blue answered, his eyes focused on the phone hanging on the wall.

Mr. Wu made a sudden rush to grab the phone ahead of Mr. Blue.

"You call the police? No. No. You no call police here."

They wrestled for the phone and Mr. Blue managed to pull it away. He began dialing.

"Mr. Wu, this is an emergency."

The commotion had reached upstairs, disturbing the rest of the house. Mrs. Wu crept down the staircase. She had on a pink silk robe, her long hair unkempt and grazing down past the small of her back. She peeked into the kitchen. Her two sons, Fai and Huan, followed closely behind her.

The phone started to ring on the other end.

"You give me back my phone and you put clothes on when you come to my home," said Mr. Wu.

Seeing the situation, Mrs. Wu stepped into the kitchen and started yelling at Mr. Wu in Chinese. He yelled back and they started talking over each other.

A voice materialized on the line: "9-1-1, what is your emergency?"

Mr. Blue put the phone up to his ear. "Hello, yes, I—"

Suddenly the phone slipped from Mr. Blue's grasp and hit the kitchen floor. Mr. Wu was gripping the phone cord in his hands, and he bent down to pick it up while Mrs. Wu continued to yell. He pulled the phone toward him and tried to hang it up, but Mr. Blue pushed him, sending him sprawling toward the cabinets. Mrs. Wu ran over to her husband, now yelling at Mr. Blue.

Mr. Blue picked up the phone from the floor and placed it against his ear again.

"Hello, 9-1-1? I need to report a crime. My house has been robbed."

Mr. Wu sat up and rubbed the back of his head while Mr. Blue caught the two boys staring at him through the kitchen walkway.

"Hello, Fai, Huan," he said, covering his privates with his hand.

The sirens made no sounds, but their lights shone bright enough to pierce the shades of every home on the block. The street outside the Blue residence was a sea of red and blue lapping at the shore of their lawn. The call had drawn the attention of almost every police officer at the local precinct. Neighbors wrapped up in robes and blankets as far as five houses away peered through their windows or stood out on their porches, looking on. It was a cold night in late November. Across the street, the Sulvich family stood huddled together outside their front door. Mr. Sulvich was kicking the screen of the door to quiet their dog, Jenny, who hadn't stopped barking since the police had shown up.

At the Blue house, Mrs. Blue sat on the porch steps, wrapped in a blanket, her eyes swollen and red. A police officer stood over her, with two other officers behind him, trying to piece the night together.

"I thought we were called in for a robbery," a thin redheaded officer whispered to the blond officer next to him.

"Keep it down," the blond officer said, elbowing him. "The mother can hear you."

A few feet away, near the sidewalk, Mr. Blue, also wrapped in a blanket, spoke with three other policemen.

"So you didn't see your son at all tonight?" asked a stout, mustached sheriff.

"No. It's like I said. I got home, my wife told me he was sick and in bed, and I didn't think anything else of it."

"You didn't think to go in to check on him?"

"No."

The other policemen looked at one another.

"What about the last time you saw him?" asked another. "Anything unusual?"

"No."

"Can you describe him for us?" asked the sheriff. "Any details that could help identify him."

"I don't know. He's got blond hair like his mother. Brown eyes like mine . . . He's just a kid, you know?"

"Age?"

"Six . . . teen? Yeah, sixteen."

"Height?"

"I don't know, about five seven, five eight? *Honey*," he called over to Mrs. Blue, pasting a smile on his face, "how tall is he?" She stared ahead, her eyes locked on the ground.

"Uh, you can go with five eight," Mr. Blue concluded.

"Can you remember anything important or out of the ordinary he may have been talking about recently? Something that could relate to his disappearance?" the sheriff asked.

"Important?" Mr. Blue looked around, as if searching for an answer. He shrugged instead. "I don't know," he mumbled.

"What don't you know?" one of the other policemen persisted.

Mr. Blue stared blankly past the officers and out into the neighbors' yard across the street. Near the side of the house, he caught the beady eyes of a deer staring back at him. Then the animal turned around and wandered into the backyard, out of view.

"I don't know the last time we talked."

The sheriff picked his head up and lowered his notepad while the other policemen shared glances of concern.

"Why don't you take it from the top? Tell us everything that happened tonight."

It was a familiar weekday evening at the Blue residence. A draft swept through the home, tightening the stitching of the leather-bound sofas in the living room. The house shuttered as the clock struck nine and the central heating system roared to life, kicking up cobwebs that hung loosely on the ventilation grills. Dinner had been prepared long ago, the first chore crossed off a short list of tasks. A stony layer of mashed potatoes caked the edges of a pot, waiting on the stove for Mr. Blue's arrival. The potatoes, along with greasy fried chicken and a side of microwaved frozen peas, had become less a tradition and more a convenience. Indifferent toward it all, Mrs. Blue took no care to cover anything in Mr. Blue's long absence.

Instead she continued her routine in front of the computer screen. A concert of clicks echoed from the downstairs computer room, and the glow of the monitor cast a beacon of light in the otherwise dark home. The monitor was a mosaic of windows from vendors willing to overnight their merchandise to her.

A car door slammed shut outside. In the past, this was Mrs. Blue's signal to minimize all windows and make herself busy, but lately she had little urge to hide anything. She hovered the mouse over the Buy Now button for a brand-new pair of high-heeled shoes, more excited about her purchase than anything else.

The front door of the house opened and Mr. Blue stepped in. He was immediately greeted by his reflection in the mirror hanging in the foyer. A mess of thinning hair had been kicked up by the howling winds outside, and his own face startled him. His eyes were sunken into their sockets, resting on a permanent line of purple and blue. His face, a mess of crow's feet and dry spots where the cold had chafed it. But just below that, his tie, made into a perfect Pratt knot, lay nestled between the collar points of his crisp white shirt. He had worn these items for years, yet they still sparkled with the same bright sheen as they had when first purchased. In them, he was a living reminder that the human body spoiled much faster than spun cotton.

He quickly looked away.

"Hello?" Mr. Blue called out into the darkness as he dropped his briefcase just outside the foyer. It hit the floor with a loud thud that reverberated through the house.

A momentary silence seized the air until Mrs. Blue crept out from the computer room, flicking on the nearest light switch to illuminate the space between them.

"You know I hate when you do that," she said, nodding toward the briefcase.

"Sorry," Mr. Blue said.

"How was your day?"

"Good."

"Oh shoot, I forgot about the food."

She made her way into the kitchen, ignoring Mr. Blue and avoiding eye contact with him. Once there, she placed her hands around the pots on the stove.

"Well, dinner is cold because you're home so late again."

Mr. Blue ignored the comment and walked back into the hall to slide the closet door open.

"Shoes *inside* the closet!" her voice called out from the kitchen.

He let out a grunt and hung his jacket while kicking his shoes inside, and then slid the door closed.

In the kitchen, Mrs. Blue popped open the microwave door and placed a plate of food inside, a paper towel on top. She closed the door, hit a few buttons, and the machine whirred to life. Mr. Blue dragged himself into the kitchen.

"Guess who I saw today?" she asked.

He let out a deep sigh. "Who did you see today?"

"I was on my way home from the supermarket and— Oh my goodness, it was such a cold day today."

The microwave beeped and Mrs. Blue opened it to check on the food. She pushed her finger into the meat and rolled her eyes, placing the plate back inside.

"Maybe if you came home a little earlier, it wouldn't be so cold," she said, scowling.

Mr. Blue opened a drawer next to the dishwasher and pulled out a large white bottle of pills. They rattled inside as he twisted the cap off, and he poured two white capsules into his palm. He threw his head back and swallowed them dry, twisting the cap on and tossing the bottle back into the drawer.

"Did you wash your hands? You look filthy. Go wash yourself, my goodness. And fix your hair."

"Are you going to finish your story or not?" Mr. Blue asked, patting down his hair.

"So anyways . . ." she started again. "I'm walking out of the supermarket and guess who I see getting into her car?"

"Who?"

"Sandy. Can you believe it? Just shopping during the day, like it's no big deal."

"Did she say hi?"

"Oh, of course she did. And of course she was out in her fancy shoes and fake designer bag. Like she has all that time to go out and shop but no time to call? Of course not."

"You should call her," Mr. Blue said as he grabbed another white bottle, shook out more pills, and then swallowed them dry.

"Oh really?" Mrs. Blue scoffed. "Call her? Oh, of course, I'll call *her*. Sandy! My best friend, Sandy. I can't wait to see *Sandy*."

Inside the microwave, the food started to pop and jump around on the plate.

"I'm not saying you need to be best friends—just say hello." Mr. Blue pressed his fingers into his temples until he could feel his veins pulsing.

"If you like her so much, how about you call? You tell her how much you want to see her. How about that?"

The popping intensified. Mrs. Blue composed herself and flung the door open, ending the whir of the machine. The contents of the plate sizzled and the skin of the chicken had turned gray, its texture like bark.

She continued to face the microwave, her back to him. "Would you go and change? I need to set the table."

Without a word, Mr. Blue made his way up the stairs to his bedroom, one heavy footstep after the next.

Two decades of working as a car salesman were taking a toll on him. For years his physical form had been deteriorating from that of a healthy, plum idealist to a pale shade that could barely stand straight. A steady flow of pills helped keep the blood pumping through his veins, but more recently his mental state had begun to decline. Suburbia wasn't the escape it used to be for Mr. Blue. Home had become a museum, dedicated to displaying a family's growing obsession with materials and a declining passion for life.

He reached the top of the stairs and made for his bedroom, down the hall. He walked past a closed door, giving it a quick glance before continuing on.

Upon entering the bedroom, he saw that the bathroom door was shut. A piece of plastic yellow tarp stuck out from underneath. Mr. Blue opened the door slowly, the tarp crumpling up against the bottom rail, to find an opened toolbox on the counter, the medicine cabinet leaning against the wall. A thin layer of dust coated the vanity. Near the bathtub, an old pair of work boots and a face mask lay on the floor.

He closed the door again and walked toward his closet. He saw his reflection once more and pulled down his collar, revealing a smear of color unlike his own on his neck. He let out a sigh, relieved that none of it had gotten on the collar.

Lately, it had become very easy to lie to Mrs. Blue. All he needed to tell her was that he had to work late for a special client and wouldn't be home until much later. And as long as the money kept coming in, the story held up and Mrs. Blue looked the other way. Sometimes it wasn't love that kept a family together but the willingness to accept things for how they were.

The smell of cigarette smoke wafted into the room and crept into his nostrils and he snapped out of it. From downstairs, he heard the back door slide open and then slide back, stopping shy of closing shut. He rubbed his nose vigorously and opened the closet door.

Mr. Blue took off his pants, and threw them into the hamper, then loosened his tie and unbuttoned his shirt. He pulled the tie through his collar and opened his tie drawer. It was an expensive tie, made of a fine cloth, in a luxurious dark navy blue. A gray logo was embroidered onto it near the very end, a man swinging a polo stick on top of a horse. In the center, a single white stripe for contrast and sophistication. It stood out from his regular assembly line of single-colored ties. It was beautiful. And it was the last time he'd ever see it.

Mrs. Blue sat on the edge of her side of the bed, moisturizing her arms and elbows. The smell of peppermint filled the air. Without warning, the bathroom door swung open and Mr. Blue appeared, startling Mrs. Blue. She glared at him.

"Would it kill you to be a little more gentle?"

"Yes."

"Wipe your feet or you'll bring dust into the bed," she said, pointing to a mat on the floor.

Mr. Blue dragged one foot after the other across the mat and then slid under the sheets. The silence was cut by the rough crinkling of the duvet, halting any further conversation.

She pushed her lotion toward the edge of the nightstand and slipped under the sheets as well. An icy, cold cave surrounded them, formed by years of eroding desires. Mr. Blue turned the TV on and flipped to his favorite news channel. The room filled with a dreary glow.

The TV repeated the same monologue as it did every night: death, destruction, disease, corruption. The stories never changed; they just got a little worse each time. But it filled the void that would otherwise be consumed by small talk or a futile effort to agree on something. No matter where they started, they always ended up cutting deeper into their open wounds. Their words were a carousel, and the monologues of misery were always the better option.

"Did you lock the front door before you came up?" Mrs. Blue asked at the commercial.

Mr. Blue hesitated, then said, "Yes."

"Are you sure? Because if I go downstairs now and check and that door isn't locked—"

Mr. Blue bit his tongue, pulling the sheets back across his body in a sweeping motion, and then made his way downstairs.

In the darkness, he could barely make out the doorknob, and the faint glow from the top of the stairs did nothing to help. His bare feet touched the cold marble foyer and he felt for the lock. There was an odd draft coming from the house, an emptiness. He thought nothing of it and kept feeling around.

To his surprise, the door was unlocked. He contemplated turning the lock as quietly and gently as possible.

Snap! The sound echoed through the house.

He trudged up the stairs once more. Again, he glanced at the closed door on his way to the bedroom, but continued on. Back under the sheets, he lay down again, keeping a distance from Mrs. Blue. To his surprise, she remained silent.

"He's been cooped up in his room all night. He's really not going to come out and say hello?" Mr. Blue asked.

"He came home early today and said he wasn't feeling well. I checked his forehead, but he didn't seem hot."

Mr. Blue sighed. "I worry about him."

"I know you do," Mrs. Blue said. "I do too."

"Sometimes I feel he will never grow up. He just locks himself in that room, doing God knows what, playing games and watching TV, just rotting his brain away. There will come a time when he has to stop. He needs to start living in the real world."

Mrs. Blue said nothing, only offering a sleepy whisper while Mr. Blue lay there in silence, placing the remote at his side as he began to doze off as well. The dreary glow lulled them to sleep, weighing down their eyelids, slipping them into their respective dreams. And then the TV turned off.

The Blue residence was a house of meticulous detail. The placement of things in each room was of the utmost importance, as if every item was meant to be an exhibit in a museum. If any of those items were to be moved without alerting Mrs. Blue, it was best to do it under the cover of night. The slightest change, the slightest misplacement, would quickly set off her internal security system. Even something as small as an unlocked door.

Around two a.m. was the usual time Mrs. Blue got up to relieve herself. On this night, at 1:07 a.m., she awoke. It was her internal security system trying to tell her something was wrong. She didn't listen. Just as gently as she'd gotten under the sheets, she slipped out and balanced herself in the darkness. With her eyes adjusted, she thought she could see the outlines of the dresser, the nightstand, and the eight-foot mirror near the walk-in closet. She tiptoed to the bathroom, the floor creaking around the bed, and curled her lip in frustration, cursing the floor under her breath.

Mrs. Blue walked into the bathroom but left the lights off. It was too much for her sensitive eyes, plus right now the bathroom was an eyesore. She stepped out onto the cold tile and carefully squatted onto the icy bowl, moving slowly to get used to the temperature. As she sat there, she looked around the empty bathroom, sliding her feet across the tile. Much like the hardwood in the bedroom, she wanted to rip up the bathroom floor too. In her mind, everything had to go: the sink, the tiles, the old showerhead. She couldn't wait to replace it all, and she blamed Mr. Blue for the state of the house, for being cheap.

She leaned forward to grab the toilet paper, but the roll was empty. She let out a groan, searching behind the toilet to grab a roll off the standing rack. But the rack was not there.

"Oh my god," she whispered.

Looking down into the blackness of the bowl, she sat for a minute, continuing to scope out the room. The next place a roll could be was the linen closet in the hallway. There were almost always extra ones there.

Mrs. Blue pulled her underwear up and tiptoed out of the bathroom and into the hallway. She opened the closet and bent down, passing by empty shelves where towels and blankets used to be. Feeling around in the darkness, she stretched her arm to the far corners of the shelf but felt nothing but wood.

"What the hell?" she muttered, standing upright.

She flicked the hallway light switch on. The white light blanketed her and she stood there for a moment, squinting. Through the blur, she thought she saw the towels and blankets exactly where they were supposed to be, but seconds later her vision cleared.

The closet was empty.

Half a dozen shelves filled with Egyptian cotton towels, silk sheets, and plush blankets made from top-brand design-ers—all gone. Her eyes widened and she thrust her arms into the closet in disbelief, touching every corner of every shelf, hoping her eyes had deceived her. But the closet was still empty, with nothing more than tufts of dust swirling around.

Confusion quickly turned to panic. She stormed into the bedroom, toward her walk-in closet. She flicked on the light switch, and more piercing white light shot back at her. Her closet, filled with an array of purses, scarves, and designer shoes—even her favorite pair with the red soles—was empty. She blinked in rapid succession, thinking it was an illusion of fatigue. But her eyes saw true. The boxes that had adorned the deep shelves, stacked on top of one another, arranged edge to edge, hanging off the sides and lining the corners of every wall, were all gone.

She let out a violent shriek that shook the house and startled Mr. Blue. He leapt from his bed and stumbled to the floor.

"What, what, what?" he yelled.

"My shoes! My dresses! My bags! They're all gone!"

Mr. Blue got to his feet and looked into the empty closet. He turned to his own closet, opening the sliding doors, and then pulled out his drawers to find them empty.

"What the hell is this?"

Mrs. Blue turned on the remaining lights in the bedroom and ran to knock on the closed door in the hallway.

"Open the door! We've been robbed!" she yelled.

There was no answer.

Mr. Blue came rushing out behind her in his underwear, and dashed down the stairs.

Mrs. Blue continued knocking on the door, but there was still no answer. Her mind raced through all the possibilities of where her belongings might have gone. Who stole them? When? How much did they steal?

"What's going on downstairs?" she yelled from the hallway. She spotted herself in the bathroom mirror across the hall and ran her fingers through her hair, straightening herself. Her satin nightgown draped just above her knees. She yanked it down.

She knocked one more time and then yelled, "Get up!" as she made her way downstairs.

Still, there was no answer at the door.

In the computer room, Mr. Blue was busy opening more drawers, revealing their emptiness. Mrs. Blue ran into the kitchen and opened up all the cupboards. They were empty as well.

"Everything is gone. Everything!" Mrs. Blue yelled. "Oh my God, oh my God," she kept repeating. "I can't believe this. . . . I can't believe . . . All my shoes!"

"Enough about the damn shoes!" Mr. Blue's voice called out from somewhere in the house.

Together they raced from room to room, cabinet to cabinet, drawer to drawer, finding each one stripped clean. There were no clocks to tell time, no phones to call the police, no keys to lock the doors. The house was empty, no longer a home of any sort.

"Call the cops!" Mrs. Blue yelled. "We have to get the police here right now."

"How can we call the cops? There're no phones!" Mr. Blue bellowed. He looked over at the wires sticking out of the telephone port in the kitchen and smacked them.

"What about your cell phone?" Mrs. Blue asked.

"What do you think?" Mr. Blue snapped back. He made for the closet and slid the door open to find his slippers.

"Empty!" he yelled, then turned around toward the front door and headed outside.

"Where are you going?" Mrs. Blue yelled. She chased after him and caught the door before it closed. "Stop! Stop! Where are you going? You can't leave me here alone. Stop!"

"Calm down!" Mr. Blue shot back at her. "Stop yelling. I'm going to the Wus' to call the police. What do you want from me?"

"Like that? You're in your underwear."

"Why don't you go inside and crochet me a pair of pants?"

Mr. Blue tiptoed across the lawn and disappeared into the darkness, leaving Mrs. Blue alone on the front porch, calling out for him. She was shaking, unsure of what was rattling her the most—her nerves or the cold.

She stopped calling for Mr. Blue and stood in the quiet darkness. Then, hesitant to do anything without him, she went back inside and shut the door behind her. The house was silent. Every breath echoed through the hall. Every creak of the floorboards sounded like the dying groans of some great beast that had been pierced by a thousand swords and left to bleed. Cabinets and drawers were open and suspended in midair, gateways to nothingness. She was afraid to walk, afraid to step any farther.

She slowly walked to the foot of the staircase and looked up toward the second floor. Then she remembered the door that was closed. The door that was *still* closed.

Inside the empty house, a team of officers and detectives scoured every room, looking for clues and evidence.

"Picked clean," one balding detective commented to a younger, taller officer. "Never seen anything like this before."

"What do you think came first? The robbery or the kidnapping?"

"I don't have the slightest clue."

The detective squatted down and shone his flashlight across the dining room floor.

"Look at the wood. Not a scratch. Not so much as a ding. You'd think the thieves would've made some marks, emptying out the house so fast," he said.

The young officer placed his hands on his hips.

"Moving rugs?" he suggested. "They could've slid the furniture out of here."

The detective stood up and flashed his light toward the front door.

"You see that?" he said as they walked over to the front door together. "Five and a half by seven feet. There's no way one guy, or guys, could've fit a dining table, a fridge, a TV"—the detective shone his light toward the different rooms of the house as he called out the objects—"or any of that stuff without so much as a scratch."

"It's like it all just . . . disappeared," the young officer proposed.

The detective raised an eyebrow at him.

Just then, another large police officer stumbled in through the front door, catching his breath.

"Hey! We found something . . . about a quarter mile away . . . Looks like dolly tracks. We're extending the perimeter!" the officer exclaimed, and practically skipped back outside, clenching the gun holster on his hip.

Many of the policemen inside the house also made a dash for the front door, leaving only a handful of older officers behind. They exchanged excited banter, eager at the possibility of a chase. The detective and the young officer stepped out onto the porch and watched as vehicles began pouring out of the neighborhood, blaring a cacophony of sirens. They gave each other a look and went back inside the house to look for more clues.

"I tell ya," the detective began, "something feels off about this one."

"What do you mean?" the young officer asked.

"I just get the feeling that there's more to this than what we're seeing."

"Like what we're *not* seeing?" the young officer suggested. The detective raised an eyebrow at him again and moved toward the back of the house.

Outside, it started to rain, and Mr. and Mrs. Blue remained sidelined as the sea of red and blue receded and police cars sped down the block.

What the officers didn't know was they were already too late. They had begun their chase for a thief who was far beyond their reach, in a place they could never find, not even in their own imaginations.

2

THE TOWER

The rain started to pick up. Arnold Blue tightened his grip on the handlebar of the steel shopping cart and pushed the Tower through the mud. The wheels of the cart cut through the muck, flinging debris at his ankles. He paid no attention to it. To his side, cars and trucks sped along the burning asphalt of the freeway, drowning out the sounds of his struggle. He was heading north, as far as he could go, until he couldn't recognize anything around him.

Across twisted highways, through lush fields, and over towering mountains separated by vast stretches of open land, Arnold pushed the Tower. From a distance, its silhouette was that of a warped spire skimming the edge of the horizon. It was a foreign structure, and it was taking its very first steps.

Arnold continued through the night, pushing and steering, even as the rain subsided and he had the opportunity to rest. Things rolled off the sides of the Tower with every bump in the road, but he paid them no mind. For now, everything was replaceable, except for the time he needed to get away.

Dawn broke and Arnold finally released his grip on the handlebar, his hands sore and red. He stared up at his creation: a fifteen-foot-tall towering monument, a collection of everything he and his family had come to own. The determination he'd felt less than twelve hours ago eclipsed all his doubts, and despite the fear and uncertainty, Arnold had achieved the impossible: he had created the Tower.

The sun peeked over the horizon. He was far enough now. Today was the first day of the rest of Arnold's life.

He collapsed to the ground, exhaustion catching up with him. He swallowed deep gulps of air as he looked up at the Tower. Just as he did, it started lurching to the side, inching toward the ground. A bright orange leather bag came tumbling down. Arnold shot up and grabbed hold of the cart, pivoting the Tower upright. Underneath the steel shopping cart was a slab of wood he'd fastened to act as a kickstand for when the Tower needed to stand on its own. He swept his foot underneath and kicked the stand into place. He backed away slowly and the Tower stood tall.

He bent down and picked up the orange bag, recognizing it immediately. The unmistakable hue stood out among the various blues and blacks back home. The grained calfskin leather had been perfectly hand-stitched and detailed with the utmost care. Even the little clochette that hung from the silver-plated handle—it was all crafted to invoke some kind of societal importance. He opened it up to find a surplus of makeup and accessories, everything from brushes to lipsticks. He turned the bag upside down and dumped its contents onto the ground. He sniffed the empty bag and breathed in deeply. It had a sweet tinge that bounced around his nostrils. It smelled as if every pleasurable moment he'd ever experienced had been crammed into a space that fit into the palms of his hands. One whiff, and he understood how addictive that smell could become. He pulled his face away and tossed the bag over his shoulder.

The rest of the day carried on this way. Items that came loose from the Tower continued to roll off the sides no matter how carefully he maneuvered. Each time it happened, it was a spectacle. Arnold played a little game in his head, counting how many times the item would roll before hitting the ground. It was the only thing keeping him from thinking too much about all the things he was losing. A swirl of emotions twisted in his stomach. A layer of guilt lay hidden just underneath his glossy eyes. It was a strange sensation he was unfamiliar with. He had to stop and sit down.

Arnold pulled a wooden plank from underneath the cart and slid it toward him. It was about the width of the cart and, when fully extended, was twice as long, just large enough for him to lie down on. Underneath the plank, he pushed another wooden kickstand into the ground. He stepped onto the plank and climbed a nearby boulder roughly twelve feet high, more than double his own height. He sat down and leaned back on his hands.

He closed his eyes and looked toward the sky to soak in the warm glow. A rush of heat pumped through his veins and he breathed out a long sigh. He tuned in to his surroundings, listening to birds chirping to one another. He opened his eyes again and watched the birds soar above him and into the distance, over the open landscape of the flatlands in front of him. He watched until the birds aligned with the sun, and he stared into it for a moment before lowering his head.

Out near the horizon, a tall, shadowy figure appeared. It was an unearthly shape, like nothing Arnold had seen before. He rubbed his eyes, trying to make it out, but the black spots in his vision from staring at the sun expanded with every blink. The figure seemed to be facing his way, remaining still. A breeze wisped by. Shivers shot down Arnold's spine. The Tower creaked and bobbed gently. He slowly got up to his feet, but as he did, the figure vanished.

"What was that?" he said, looking at the Tower as if it might answer. Then he stared back toward the horizon.

He hopped down and searched inside the Tower, pulling out a pair of sunglasses. These were his father's, and badly scratched, perhaps by some object in the Tower they had grinded up against. He slid the glasses on and looked to the horizon once more. The figure was still nowhere to be seen.

"A mirage," he thought out loud.

The unfamiliar terrain started to close in on him, and he was feeling claustrophobic. He thought it best to keep on. The world felt less like what he had seen on television and more like what he had seen in his imagination. It was unnerving, but not enough to stop him. He wanted to see more.

After three days of traveling, Arnold found a map inside the Tower and used it to trace a path north from his hometown. During the happiest parts of his childhood, he and his family had taken frequent summer road trips to beaches and lake houses. In those times, a paper map was their greatest asset for finding their way. Now, after years of neglect, the map had faded. He tried to quantify what three days of stop-and-go looked like, but there was no real way of knowing, so he folded the map and tore it into pieces. If he was going to fully commit himself, he had to eliminate any potential temptations to turn around. He knew that if there were an opportunity to go back, he would eventually give in. Without the map to navigate his way home, he had no other choice but to keep moving forward. He would follow his path north and trust in his decision.

"Rises in the east, sets in the west, right?" he asked the Tower.

Again, it gave no answer.

From the beginning, the Tower required a lot of Arnold's attention. When the road became harsh, a loose can or a remote to one of the Blue televisions tumbled down the side. He always had to be on the lookout for objects threatening to fall on him.

This became very clear when, during a particularly steep climb up a hill, Arnold noticed a corner of a blanket poking out of the Tower. Curious, he pulled at it, unhinging a toaster that crashed down, just missing his head.

If he was going to make it much farther without breaking any bones, he would have to pick through the Tower carefully. The Tower was like a newborn puppy; it had to learn how to walk beside him and he had to learn how to coexist with it. But despite the rough start, the Tower held—and the only real test, Arnold found, challenged his own psyche.

Just a few days removed from home, uncertainty crept into the crevices of his mind. Every item that fell from the Tower invoked a memory he couldn't help but reminisce about. Things he had collected over the years and forgotten suddenly gained new life—old picture books he used to thumb through when he was a child, toys of block men he'd built castles for, CDs of old games that didn't run properly on his current computer, a shoebox of old photos from elementary school. They all found salvation from a lifetime buried in dust, thanks to the Tower.

Arnold sat in the dirt and sifted through the items, confronting the memories of each one, paying his respects to a past he had chosen to run away from. He realized that *these* items made the Tower feel like a friend. It was the other things, the things that belonged to his parents, that made the anger in him burn bright. The feeling of nostalgia was strong, and he hadn't prepared for these conflicting emotions. He thought he could ride forward with nothing but anger in him, but he was wrong.

The flatlands he traversed now gave way to smooth hills. After that, the ground became flat again, with more vegetation and grass. He came around the bend of a particularly rocky section, descending to the flat, grassy plains. Just a few inches into the field, the Tower stalled, eating up chunks of grass in every wheel. With the abrupt stop, the handlebar of the cart jammed into him. He let out a grunt and rubbed his chest, then swept his foot under the cart to dig the kickstand into the ground.

"Ouch." He looked up at the Tower, as if expecting some sort of apology.

With the Tower parked, Arnold walked to the side of the cart and kneeled down.

"Dirt, grass, weeds . . . everything's in here," he declared with a groan.

The Tower creaked.

He dug a finger in between the wheel and the metal plates bolted to each side and flung away some of the caked-on muck, surprised at how easily it had compacted. He saw now that the plates were not secured as tightly as they should have been.

He stood up and walked to the back of the Tower, reaching underneath the cart to pull out part of the plank. The Tower creaked again and swayed as he got on top of the flat sheet of wood. A breeze swept by. The sun hung low in the sky, halfway through its descent toward the horizon. Up inside the Tower, he saw a piece of red metal sticking out. The unmistakable red hue belonged to his father's toolbox.

He grabbed hold of the Tower and planted his foot into the side. Like shoveling into a pile of fresh snow, his foot created a notch that held firm. He pulled himself up and started climbing toward the toolbox. The handle came within reach. Arnold tugged at it, but it barely moved. He climbed up a little higher and grabbed it with both hands now, bracing himself and channeling all his strength into his forearms. The toolbox flung out of the Tower and smacked him above his eye. Papers and other stationery items came loose as he fell backward onto the grass, the toolbox bursting open onto the ground next to him. He lay there, rubbing the spot above his eye, which was numb and bleeding, and wiped his blood on the grass.

As the dust settled, a cluster of tools lay strewn all over the ground. He looked back up at the Tower and at what was now a large hole in the side of it. On his feet again, he climbed up toward the hole. He reached the edge of it, where the toolbox had lain dormant, and hoisted himself up inside. As long as he didn't lean back, the space was just wide enough for him to sit in and dangle his legs over the edge.

He looked out at the sky as it transformed into a spiraling canvas of cotton candy. The wind whipped up again and the Tower swayed. He held on to it tightly, afraid it would tip over. But it held its ground, the brake in place, and continued only to sway. A calming sensation took over. The Tower assured Arnold it was okay to let go, and he loosened his grip.

A sting on his hand drew his attention and he pulled it to his face. A number of fresh scratches on his knuckles were bleeding. He wasn't sure when he had gotten them, but he wiped the accumulated blood onto his pants and rubbed his fingers along the open flesh. He smirked and breathed in deeply, looking back out into the distance. There was a certain electricity in the air, something he couldn't describe but felt intensely. For a moment he forgot about the jammed wheels and the mess of tools below. He forgot about the pain above his eye and the scratches on his hand. About the conflict within himself. It was a moment he wanted to remember. A moment he could come back to.

He looked around at the hole he'd created. The walls of the hole were a blur, with specks that shone back at him. Picture frames and plastic bags with big yellow smiley faces on them poked out. All the objects in the walls were held in place tightly under the weight of the Tower.

Arnold turned his body around and climbed down from his perch. He hopped off the plank and dusted off his hands, looking back up at the hole.

Suddenly it hit him.

He began scanning the Tower high and low, looking for a clue as to where to dig. He circled it—once, twice, three times—until finally he saw it.

There, between the Weedwacker and a spare tire, a piece of bright yellow plastic poked through a corner, near the front of the Tower where the top grate of the shopping cart ended. It was the tarp that had been covering the floor of his parents' bathroom during the renovation. He wrapped his hand around it and pulled it toward him. It didn't budge. He tried again, and still nothing.

Too bad. This would really come in handy next time it rains, Arnold thought. *And that perch is the perfect place to keep it.*

He let out a long sigh.

He still had wheels to fix.

After a week away from home, Arnold was beginning to feel the effects of living in the wild. His blond hair was coated with a thick layer of grease. Dirt caked under his fingernails, and his clothes were stained with spots of mud, grass, and oils from the boxed foods he had been consuming. He pined for a fresh shirt and a shower, a real bed with fresh sheets. His journey away from home was slowly transitioning into a journey toward the first town in which he could find rest. He wiped grease from his forehead and held on to the hope that at any moment the horizon would give way to civilization.

He looked down at his watch. It was almost noon as he pushed the Tower through some dry lands. The soil was tinged a sand-like color from the sun and lack of rain. He came around a bend of a hill and again caught a glimpse of the yellow tarp peeking out, teasing him. He glared at it, frustrated with himself for realizing too late that he might need it. Up inside the perch he had created days ago, the toolbox still lay. Every bump rattled the tools in the box, reminding him that if the Tower broke down, he had what he needed to try to fix it.

He decided to rest for lunch, and positioned the Tower to shade him from the sun. He swept his foot underneath the cart and dug the brake into the dry soil. As he walked the perimeter, he shook the Tower every couple of steps to check its stability, and then walked back to pull out the plank. He hopped on top and sat down, resting his back against the cart. Tied to the grates was a backpack he'd filled with food he had found inside the Tower over the past seven days. He unzipped it and pulled out a half-eaten bag of pretzels, a jar of peanut butter, and a can of soda. He cracked open the can and took a big gulp, reeling from the intense fizz.

Leaning back, he looked up at the Tower and watched it sway gently in the breeze. A shiver ran down his spine, and his cheeks turned red. The looming height of the Tower placed a strange sensation inside him. Unsure of why, he set his sights out onto the land in front of him. The silence was strangely satisfying, even after being away from civilization for so long. Perhaps, with the Tower at his back, he felt a bit more safe.

But the silence didn't last long. In the distance, he heard faint chatter. Three figures walking in tandem quickly approached him: two tall ones, with a shorter one between them. Arnold packed away his lunch and zipped up the backpack before getting to his feet. One of the figures waved to him.

"Hey, buddy!" a male voice called out.

Arnold's ears perked up. It was the first voice other than his own that he had heard in a week. As the figures approached, he could make them out better. It was a man, a woman, and a little girl, all carrying large rucksacks.

"Hey," the man called out again. "Hello there."

Arnold waved back at the man.

"Hey, good afternoon to ya," the man said, out of breath from speed walking. "Whoa, what in the world is that?"

The three travelers looked up at the Tower.

"It's a . . . Well, it's . . . It's a . . . It's pretty cool, huh?" Arnold replied, unsure of what exactly to call it.

"Pretty cool? More like pretty strange," the man replied. "Where'd you find that thing?"

"Didn't find it," Arnold said as he hopped off the plank. "Made it. Myself."

"Wow, made it. Now *that* is cool," the man continued, still out of breath. "What are you doing out here?"

"Just taking a break."

"I see. We're heading east, toward the sea. Taking this one to see the ocean for the first time."

The man attempted to nudge the little girl out from behind the woman's legs, but she held on to them tightly.

"Where *you* headed to?" the man asked.

"North. Looking for a place to settle in hopefully," Arnold replied.

The woman finally spoke. "Have you thought about traveling east?"

Just as she did, their daughter peeked out from behind the woman's legs. She had long dark-orange hair that was braided in pigtails, and she was wearing a faded pink dress. Arnold looked at her for a brief moment, then turned away.

"I have," he said. "But north is where I'm going."

"That's a shame," the man said, fidgeting with the straps of his backpack. "It's hard traveling alone out here. People are the best resource you got when traveling, ya know?"

"I'm not sure I agree," Arnold said, pointing to the Tower. "The best resource for me is right there. And more useful than any person I can think of."

Arnold paused for a moment.

"Are you low on resources?"

The man briefly looked down, then back at Arnold. "It's been a rough few days."

Arnold thought of all the food he knew was still somewhere inside the Tower. With everything he had cleared out of the pantries and fridge back home, there was enough food to last for weeks.

"I'm sorry," Arnold mumbled, unable to look any of them in the face.

"Come again?" the man asked.

Arnold looked over at his backpack filled with food. He was beginning to understand that letting go wasn't the same for everything in the Tower. He needed the food, just like he needed the tools above him and the tarp still trapped inside. But the Tower was also filled with things he didn't need, things he would gladly give away and not think twice about. It was all starting to blend together into one thing: the Tower. Separating the irreplaceables from the disposables was difficult for Arnold to understand. He didn't want to part with anything that might cripple his support in this new world. The thought terrified him.

"I said I'm sorry. I wish I had something I could offer you," Arnold finally answered.

Just then the little girl broke free from behind her mother's legs and ran up to the Tower, placing a hand on it. She smiled up at Arnold, revealing a wide grin with a few missing teeth. Across her face were splotches of dry dirt. Much like him, they had likely been wandering outdoors for days. The innocence in her eyes mirrored what remained in his.

The woman moved behind the little girl and scooped her up. "Sorry. We'll be on our way now," she said, waving the man over.

"Well, take care, young man. Hope wherever you're headed is kind to ya," he said, his head drooping.

The travelers passed Arnold and turned to wave at him as he did the same. He watched as they kicked up dust off the ground, creating a thin screen of smoke around their ankles. Arnold focused on their daughter. It was easier to look at her while she was facing away. Her innocence conjured a whirlwind of confusing emotions inside him.

He had to fight the feeling of wanting to hold on to everything in the Tower.

"Wait!" he called out.

Arnold ran toward the travelers and waved for them to stop and come back. He ran to the Tower and jumped up onto the plank, digging his hands inside.

The three returned, watching Arnold run circles around the Tower, pulling out every manner of boot, sneaker, and shoe. He pulled out footwear of all shapes and colors and placed them on the ground, lined up in rows of two. A dozen shoes quickly became a dozen pairs. Heels with polished soles and sequin-encrusted pumps next to black leather oxfords and multicolor-laced sneakers.

"What are you doing?" the man finally asked.

Arnold stood at the head of the row of shoes as if he were leading a march. "This is for you," he said. "For you and your family."

The man and the woman looked at each other, then back at the shoes.

"Oh . . . thanks . . . but we don't need these. We've got the shoes on our feet to last us," the woman said.

"It's a long journey to the sea," Arnold replied. "What if you encounter some rough terrain on your way there?"

The woman looked over at a pair of red-soled high heels. "But these aren't walking shoes," she said.

Arnold looked down. "I know . . . I just . . . This is all I can give right now," he said with a halfhearted smile.

He stood there for a moment, waiting for their response, but the family of travelers said nothing. Arnold looked at the little girl, who was too preoccupied with the shoes to look back at him. She seemed happier now.

He walked to the Tower, giving a final "Good luck" to the travelers, and kicked up the brake. The Tower shook to life and he heaved it forward.

The family, still not entirely sure of what to do, stood side by side, hand in hand, watching Arnold leave. The rows of shoes stood at attention, some old, some new. The little girl walked over to them and squatted down next to a pair of blue sequined sandals a few sizes too big.

"Don't touch them," the woman called to her. "Who knows where they've been?"

"That was strange, wasn't it?" the man asked. "Are we just going to leave them here?"

"I don't know. Check them. Maybe we can take one pair," the woman said.

The travelers glanced over the different pairs of shoes. The woman settled on bright yellow-and-white sneakers, while also carefully placing the pair of red-soled high heels into her pack while the man was looking away. The man took a pair of brown moccasins, and their daughter, who had made up her mind a while ago, took the blue sequined sandals, slipping them on and finding her balance.

"Honey, those are too big," the woman said to her daughter.

She looked at her feet, then up at the woman, her eyes wide.

"Okay, just . . . hold my hand so you don't fall," the woman said.

Then they continued on their journey, leaving the rest of the shoes behind.

When he was far away from the family, Arnold parked the Tower and sat down next to it. He picked up a stick and started drawing lines in the dirt. He felt embarrassed for what he had done. The shoes were an attempt to make him feel better about himself, but he didn't feel better at all. The ones that the travelers wouldn't take were doomed to spend the rest of their days baking in the sun, until time buried them in dust forever. He felt bad for dooming them. He wanted to turn back and pick up whatever they hadn't taken, but he knew he had to resist. The urge to hold on to every little thing inside the Tower was something he had to fight.

The sun settled at its highest point in the sky as he and the Tower moved on.

"There was a sale."

That was always the excuse. Those red price tags may as well have been a matador's red cape in Mrs. Blue's mind, and she, the charging bull. It didn't matter if it was her third pair of the week. It didn't matter if the last three pairs were still collecting dust in the closet. All that mattered was the sale. She'd sell her soul for a good deal.

But Arnold never thought she wasn't deserving of the purchase; it was just that it always took priority over everything else. It could've been anything, really: shoes, bags, clothes, drugs. It was all there to fill a void. That was the part he couldn't stand.

She chose to let the worst parts of herself flourish. Arnold never accepted that. She was supposed to be his role model, someone to look up to in the face of all that life would throw at him. Instead she became a constant reminder of the consequences of failing to create a life worth living.

The day came when Arnold had to do something about it. So he stole every pair of shoes she'd ever owned and forced her to do something about it too.

3

TO KINGDOM

The giant observation wheel in the distance made revolutions that spun in his pupils. It invoked in Arnold memories of summers spent in the converted parking lot of his high school, made to look like a carnival. On those hot summer nights, he would roam the grounds, drifting from ride to ride, looking to fall in love with any girl who would show him the slightest attention. While swirling around in the Tilt-A-Whirl, his mind would often find its way to the Ferris wheel towering over the carnival. There he would envision himself, sitting next to any number of those girls he had fallen in love with. After so many faces that had turned away, he could never clearly see the girl he wanted.

He snapped out of it. The wheel he saw now, peeking out from the horizon, was easily a twenty-mile walk, maybe more; he couldn't tell for sure. Ahead of him were more flatlands, making for an easy trek for him and the Tower. The harsh lands and rough terrain he'd traversed up to this point had helped to solidify the Tower, compacting it into a tighter shape, like a ball of tinfoil that had been squeezed harder and harder. It was no longer the loosely thrown together object Arnold had created in darkness.

In the days since he had crossed paths with the family of travelers, letting go of parts of the Tower hadn't gotten any easier. Just the thought of destroying things that held so many memories filled him with guilt, and he tried his best to ignore the moments when he wanted to burn the Tower to the ground and be done with it. The memories seemed to have a hold on him, as if they were invoking the wrath of his family and punishing him. He tried his best to stay motivated in getting as far away from home as possible.

The giant observation wheel in the distance did a good job of distracting him now.

What a strange place for that to be, so far from home, he thought.

It was the first discernible sign of civilization he'd seen in over a week. If he were lucky, there would be a place he could shower and rest—a place where he could map out the rest of his journey, both for himself and the Tower. He stared at the horizon and kept marching on.

Years ago, Arnold and his father had attended a car show down south, in a city near the coast. Its streets lined with lampposts on cobblestone roads that had been paved over hundreds of years ago. The city and its lights were in stark contrast to the marshlands surrounding it, and together they created nothing more than a hole carved into mud, artificially created to show-case machines made from fire and metal.

Arnold's father attended these shows at least once a year with Mrs. Blue. Every time he invited Arnold to come along, Arnold found an excuse to get out of it: an important school project, a lie about a classmate's birthday, or faking an illness. The last thing Arnold wanted to do was be alone with his father for a long period of time. Their constant tension was only made worse when it was just the two of them.

The year Arnold finally joined his father was the year his mother had to stay with a friend who was sick and not doing well. It took a lot of convincing and days of arguments, but his mother finally decided to go on her own, and Arnold agreed to take her place on his father's trip.

Mr. Blue needed to attend shows like these, as they were where he made most of the connections necessary to fill his lot with new cars every year. The floor shows, held in the ballrooms of fancy hotels, were littered with attractions. There was always some sales rep showing off a flashy new car, and an attractive woman straddling it, luring men into spending their money.

On the showroom floor, Arnold and his father made fre-quent stops to shake hands with men in suits, and Mr. Blue only periodically introduced Arnold to them. Once they started talk-ing business, though, Arnold tuned them out.

The event was supposed to last all day, but after about three hours, Arnold could barely fake his interest anymore.

"You okay? You want to go back to the room?" his father asked.

Arnold hesitated to respond right away.

"I thought we would find a booth with some cool cars. Maybe you'll see something you might like?"

"Sure."

"Or you can go back to the room."

"I can stay if you want me to," Arnold said.

"Let's check out a few more panels and then you can head up. Okay?"

"Okay."

After about thirty minutes, Arnold went up to their hotel room. As the door shut, he was greeted with an immediate sense of calm. The plush carpets soaked up all the noise around him, except, of course, for the noise in his head.

He slipped off his shoes and slid into a chair at the corner table in the soft glow of the bedroom lights. On the table he dropped a few small bags he had brought back from the showroom floor, filled with trinkets: key chains, paperweights, pens, notepads, and other things that companies had printed their logos on.

He emptied the bags out onto the table and started organizing them. He laid out all the pens together in one pile, then stacked together all the notepads, key chains, and so on.

He sat at the table in silence, mulling over the piles of junk. Then, through the window, he heard the sounds of laughter. He pulled the thick curtains to the side and looked down at the beach lining the coast. The moon was reflected onto the ocean, turning the dark water into bright white ripples cascading onto the shore.

Back and forth.

Back and forth.

He felt himself swaying with them.

Just at the shoreline, he made out a group of teenagers sitting in a circle, three guys and two girls. One was playing the guitar while the others sang along and passed around a bottle of brown liquid. Arnold sat down on the edge of the bed closest to the window and watched them smile and listened to them sing, unable to look away from the spaces left open in between them.

He fell backward onto the bed and breathed out a long sigh. Then he closed his eyes, drifting off, longing to hear the plucking of a guitar in his ear alongside waves crashing onto the shore.

He awoke sometime later to the clicking sounds of the door opening. It slammed shut, and Arnold rolled his eyes in frustration.

"Oops, sorry. You awake?" Mr. Blue asked.

"I was just lying down. How was the rest of the show?" Arnold asked as he moved again to the corner table.

"Good. It was good," Mr. Blue said, immediately loosening his tie and unbuttoning his shirt.

"Make any new connections?"

"A few. Yeah."

Mr. Blue emptied out his pockets, and a swath of business cards rained down onto the table on top of Arnold's neatly arranged piles.

"Sorry."

Mr. Blue picked up the cards and pushed them aside, knocking into the pile of notepads, and sat down across from him at the table.

"What do we got?" Mr. Blue asked.

"Just some junk."

Mr. Blue glanced over the piles. "This is kind of cool."

In the pile of one-off items that Arnold had put together, Mr. Blue picked out a pocket compass. It was light blue and made from some kind of cheap plastic. On the back it read, UNLIMITED SERVICE, the name of the company that had been handing them out.

"Here," he said, handing it to Arnold. "Keep it for when you need some direction."

Then Mr. Blue let out a sarcastic chuckle that transformed into a clenched fist, jabbing Arnold in the gut.

Arnold refocused on the giant observation wheel, which was much closer now. He could just start to make out the spinning motion of it, as the light from the sun reflected off it and shone back at him. He looked down at his compass, reading a bearing between north and northwest. To his surprise, the compass still worked after almost two years of sitting in his bedroom drawer. Now it served as his only real road map.

At about five miles out, he guessed, he could more clearly see what he was approaching. It was a town, but one that resembled a carnival. There were tents of all colors as far as he could see, flags waving in the wind, balloons floating up into space, and more giant wheels than he could count. The one he had been staring at, as it turned out, wasn't even the biggest one. But it still towered over any he had seen before, by at least three times. It rotated slowly, like a cog in a machine, and as he got closer he heard it creak and moan like a bellowing whale. It made the looming height of the Tower feel insignificant.

His ears perked up at the faint sound of music, the frantic plucking of guitar strings, the clapping of tambourines, and the blaring of wooden pipes.

An overwhelming sensation came over him, the familiar feeling of yearning for acceptance but also wanting to run away.

He veered the Tower off to the side and started his route around the town. As he walked, the music grew louder and he stopped in his tracks. He took a few deep breaths and shook out his hands before turning the Tower around. The new Arnold wouldn't let something like fear control his actions. The Tower was a reminder that he had been brave before.

Aside from the giant observation wheel in front of him, there was no formal entrance or closed gate stopping him from wandering into the town. He pushed the Tower forward through a large open field. Concrete benches and worn-down fountains punctuated his path, though the fountains clearly hadn't been operating for some time. There was an eerie quietness where he was, despite the music and noise he heard not too far off. The field was bordered by a fence with a gate that opened up into a cul-de-sac lined with town house–type homes. Only, the homes weren't made from conventional materials like wood and stone. Upon further examination, Arnold noticed they were made from cloth, like a circus tent stitched to mimic the outline of a house.

He approached a house at the end of the cul-de-sac that was shaded by a very large oak tree. After a quick survey of the area, he pushed the Tower next to the side of the house and kicked back the brake. He shook the Tower a few times to check its sturdiness and then walked to the front of the house. The steps leading up to the stoop were made from crudely nailed wooden planks, and the door was just a cloth sheet tied at two corners and along the sides. He walked up the creaky steps and stood facing the door.

"Uhh," he couldn't help but mutter.

He pulled his hand up to knock but unclenched his fist as the door fluttered in the wind.

"Hello?"

No answer.

He tried to peek through the stitching but could see only darkness inside.

"Hellooo?" he called out again.

Still no answer.

He backed away and looked out into the neighborhood. There was no trace of anyone. He went back around the side of the house to the Tower. The oak tree covered most of the Tower's side with its large branches and abundant foliage. He wanted to make sure the town was safe before he went around hauling a fifteen-foot-tall target through the streets.

A swathe of gray clouds loomed overhead. He walked to the front of the Tower, where the bright yellow tarp was still poking out. He gripped it and pulled with both hands. It hardly budged.

"How mad would you be if it rained?" he joked to the Tower. "Me too."

Now he twisted the piece of tarp around one hand and firmly grasped it. Using his other hand, he reached under the cart for leverage and pulled down hard, twisting and gyrating from side to side until his palm burned like fire.

Still nothing.

He let go and eyed the Tower from top to bottom. He realized that if he was going to free the tarp at some point, he'd have to lessen the weight bearing down on it.

Next time, he thought.

He swallowed the lump in his throat and headed into town. Walking along the sidewalk, he peeked into some of the houses he passed. But just like the first house, all he could see was darkness. No one was home.

He picked up the faint smell of something sweet in the air, a puzzling combination of tanginess mixed with grease and dried sweat. The air became thicker too, and it was a little harder to breathe as he got closer to the source of the music. On the corner of the sidewalk, a street sign caught his attention. No name, no letters or markings to pinpoint where he was. Instead the entire sign was painted a reddish-brown color. He didn't know what to make of it.

A few blocks down, the source of the music was close enough to be overshadowed by the sounds of children and loud but indistinct chatter. He peered through a thick patch of bushes and saw what looked like a festival: a sprawling scene of children, families, food stands, tapestry, and colorful balloons. Some children roamed from stand to stand in groups, while others held hands with their mothers, their free hands holding treats like hot dogs or ice cream. There was a group of four rather large men sitting on folding chairs in a semicircle. In the middle, there was a table with a mountain of chicken wings. Each man wore a utility belt with half a dozen pouches hanging on each hip. Before every bite, they would dip a piece of chicken into a pouch, and it would emerge covered in a thick amber liquid. Farther down, he saw a rotund blond-haired boy trying to wrestle a piece of jerky out of a dog's mouth. The dog was also fairly large in size. The boy ultimately lost when his greasy hands could no longer keep a grip on the jerky.

The strange smell was much stronger now, and the air seemed to weigh on Arnold even more. A loud series of ringing noises sounded a few stands away, and a flock of plump adults and children waddled toward it. Arnold emerged from the bushes, trying to act natural and draw as little attention to himself as possible. He dusted his pants off, sharing polite smiles with the people who walked past him. Not one of them so much as glanced his way.

Another succession of rings sounded off at the stand next to him, though its tune was slightly different from the one before. A few adults and children broke off from the group of people heading to the first stand, and formed a line. A portly man wearing a brown suit and a brown cowboy hat emerged holding a nearly six-foot-tall cart of steaming chicken wings. He began throwing a dozen at a time into brown paper bags, then held the bags out for people to take. One by one, people grabbed the bags and receded to the nearby benches to eat.

More rings sounded off in the distance. But unlike the previous ones, this ringing was different, including two short dings, a pause, and then five more quick dings. Arnold thought the sounds might be a signal to let people know food was available at a particular stand. He merged into the main group heading to one of the stands. Still, no one noticed him.

As the crowd approached another stand, Arnold veered off to the side to watch, hearing children shout in excitement, "Look, it's him, it's him!" They were all greeted by a table topped with a pyramid of sliced sandwiches. Behind it, a very large man with a wide grin stood proud, his chest and belly out. Above him, a big yellow sign read:

MCFULTY'S SANDWICH SHOP

McFulty wore blue-jean overalls that hugged every lump on his body. He had a long gray beard that whisked down onto his chest, and a handlebar mustache that rose over his plump cheeks. His looks were rivaled only by his demeanor as he raced back and forth with the spunk of a teenager. McFulty began handing out sandwiches left and right, rubbing little children's heads and calling out to older folks by their first names. He drew in the crowd, and Arnold began to feel the effects as he found himself inching closer to the front. Before he knew it, he was next in line for a sandwich.

"Okay, who do we got next? Yes, yes, plenty for everyone. Don't be shy now," McFulty rambled as he reached into the crowd, a plate of sandwiches in both hands. "Here ya go, big ol' plate for ya."

He turned his head toward Arnold as his other arm was stretched out to a plump little boy. He did a double take and locked his eyes on Arnold, releasing his grip on both plates. Arnold jumped forward and grabbed one plate out of midair, but the little boy wasn't so lucky. The entire plate fell onto his face and shirt in a colorful display of meats and sauces. The boy's eyes welled up and he ran away through the legs of the crowd. There was a hush. Arnold stood, frozen.

"Oh, I—I, uh—" Arnold stuttered.

"Whoops, sorry about that, folks!" McFulty exclaimed. "Old age just kinda does that to ya sometimes. Haha, lost my grip there for a second. Everybody look this way, though. Plenty of sandwiches to go around. Don't be shy now, c'mon."

Quickly, the silence was filled as McFulty corralled the crowd back into a frenzy. He got the attention away from the accident almost immediately, using the sandwiches as a distraction. He glared at Arnold as he continued to dole out sandwiches, which Arnold took as his cue to leave. He faded into the background as the wave of hungry customers pushed forward.

Away from the crowd he found an empty bench to sit on, tucked behind some bushes. He looked down at his plate of sandwiches. They were oddly shaped, cut into long, oval slices. Arnold inspected the filling of each one as he pondered the odd reaction he'd received from McFulty, a total stranger. Out of all the people he had walked by, for some reason he was the only one to take notice. And not just take notice—take offense, almost.

He flipped over one of the sandwiches. They didn't look that appealing.

"Why all the commotion?" he whispered to himself as he pressed his finger down into the spongy white bread. A bright yellow liquid oozed from between the slices.

He looked up at the sky, at the mountain of gray clouds billowing ever closer. They seemed to expand right over him. He worried about the Tower and how exposed it was. He used that thought to convince himself that perhaps there was nothing for him in this town. He felt disconnected from everything going on, a feeling he was familiar with. But now it was more than just a feeling. Everyone had ignored him.

The wind began to pick up. His hair fluttered onto his forehead and he let it sit there for a few seconds before brushing it to the side. He rubbed his fingers together and smelled them. It had been days since he'd last bathed.

Maybe I'll just spend one night and leave in the morning, he thought.

His stomach grumbled as he spread apart one of the sandwiches. A few more bells went off in the distance, and he watched through the bushes as families scurried down the street. Above him, he heard the creaking turnstiles of a mammoth-sized wheel. It moaned with every revolution. The carts that normally occupied the wheels in his memories, the ones that could only hold two people at a time, were now giant glass domes the size of a house. As each dome reached ground level, the wheel stopped for about fifteen minutes to let people off and let a new group of people on board.

Arnold scarfed down his plate of sandwiches, enjoying them more than he thought he would. Then he headed toward the great wheel to get a better look. On the way, he passed McFulty's stand again. The crowd had thinned noticeably since he'd left, and McFulty was nowhere to be seen.

He passed a market selling different kinds of chocolates, and kicked at a bunch of wrappers strewn about the street. Past the market, he entered a pathway flanked by bushes on either side, leading to the great wheel. From here, he saw more great wheels in the distance and a crowd of at least a hundred people.

His fingers grazed the bushes and he pulled a leaf off a stem, folding and crumpling it in his hands. He opened his hand again, and the bits of leaf floated into the wind and disappeared.

He was now as close as he could get to one of the great wheels, and from this distance, it seemed as tall as a skyscraper. Next to the dome-shaped carts was a platform that people lined up on, waiting for the next cart to descend. He made his way around the line, trying to get a glimpse of what was inside the domes as people began moving up single file, but all he could see was a white light that enveloped everyone who walked inside. Then the dome sealed shut and the wheel began its revolution again.

He looked over at an old man waiting in line, and tried to make eye contact, but the man didn't even look his way. He contemplated tapping him on the shoulder for more information, but decided not to, feeling deflated by the lack of attention. He started his way back to where he'd left the Tower.

Arnold traced his steps toward the pathway flanked by bushes. He was brushing his fingers along the leaves again when, suddenly, an arm burst out from behind them, grabbing Arnold by his collar. He jumped, startled, clamping his hand around the attacker's wrist as another arm sprang free, grabbing a handful of Arnold's shirt. After a few moments of struggling, Arnold was pulled into the bushes, where he fell out the other side onto something soft and cushioned. A person. Arnold rolled off his attacker and onto the grass, landing on his back.

"Are you crazy?" the attacker exclaimed as he stumbled to his feet.

"Am *I* crazy?" Arnold yelled back, propping himself onto his elbows and looking up. It was McFulty.

"You can trust me," McFulty assured Arnold as he stood at the mouth of a drainpipe leading into a dark tunnel. "If there's anyone you need to trust now, it's me."

Under any other circumstance, Arnold would have never believed the words of a stranger who had, just minutes ago, grabbed and thrown him onto the ground. He would also not follow that same stranger into a drainage pipe. But Arnold did not feel threatened by McFulty. He felt strangely connected to him, like he had met him before or known him for a long time.

"Where are we going?" Arnold asked.

"Somewhere safe," McFulty assured him.

"Am I in danger?"

"Not if you stick with me."

As Arnold stepped into the tunnel, his foot splashed into a shallow pool of water. He lifted his foot up and looked at the thick, murky puddle.

"The ground is a lot less wet the farther in you go," McFulty said.

Arnold gave a nod and continued to follow him.

"This had to happen eventually," McFulty muttered to himself. "You did this to yourself. It was only a matter of time."

"Excuse me?" Arnold asked.

"Nothing, just . . . talking to myself, is all. The name's McFulty. Morgan McFulty. Everyone here calls me by my last name though. It's a name that people here trust. It's my brand. What's your name?"

"Arnold."

"Arnold what?"

"Blue."

"Arnold Blue," McFulty repeated. "Keep up, Arnold Blue. You don't want to get left behind down here."

Arnold continued to follow McFulty through the tunnel, periodically stopping each time he began muttering to himself again.

"Have to get him out of here as soon as possible. The festival is almost over. . . ." he kept repeating.

Arnold was no stranger to being in a place where he was unwanted. From early on in school, he had become a favorite target for bullies.

"Hey, Arnold, think fast," he would hear as a freshly spit-soaked wad of paper pelted him in the back of the head. A cascade of laughter would follow from the handful of boys sitting behind him.

They were the cosmos hurling meteors at him.

In those moments, "think fast" meant the same to him as "don't move." Arnold was always more afraid to stand up for himself than he was of what the boys might do to him. Even during those brief moments when he was able to muster up the courage to confront them, he pushed it back down inside, burying it deeper and deeper. Arnold told himself it was easier to wait for the boys to finish and move on to something else, and then he would be left alone again.

He would spend the rest of those days in the bathroom cleaning spitballs out of his hair, finding them stuck to his shirt or in his pockets.

But even still, despite the times he was forced to be the center of a universe he wanted no part in, they were still better than the days when he was so ignored and so left alone, it was as if he didn't exist.

Late at night, he would stare up at his bedroom ceiling and replay the day in his head. Arnold couldn't shake the feeling that one day he would stand up for himself—except, it wouldn't be his decision. The only way it would happen was if he was so cornered that his only option would be to fight. The day would come, the thought echoed in his mind, and it would have nothing to do with his own courage.

They approached a fork in the tunnel, and McFulty continued to the left without pause. The path ahead was overrun with wild vegetation covering most of the roughly eight-foot-high steel pipe. The old pipes they were traveling through seemed to be tunnels that might have once been used to transport waste or other resources around the town.

"Not too many people know these tunnels exist anymore," McFulty said, as if reading Arnold's mind.

Light flooded the corridor ahead. McFulty walked toward it and crouched down, calling Arnold over. Arnold soon realized that the light was pouring in through a steel grate. He looked up as McFulty pointed toward the sky.

"Ever seen something so amazing?" he asked.

Arnold inched closer to McFulty to get a better look. A great wheel towered above them. The massive dome cabins reached toward the sky with each revolution.

The tunnel suddenly went dark and Arnold flinched.

"Don't be afraid," McFulty assured him. "The darkness is your ally."

"What do you mean?"

"Out of sight, out of danger," McFulty said with a smile. It seemed forced, much less genuine than the McFulty who had been happily handing out sandwiches earlier.

Arnold squinted at him. The tunnel filled with light again as the dome cabin moved past the grate. McFulty started walking again.

"C'mon, let's keep moving."

Arnold followed closely behind. McFulty was a lot quicker and more spry than Arnold had expected for a man his size. His belly hung out the sides of his overalls and extended about half an arm's length, and his thighs rubbed together with every step.

After a few more minutes Arnold stopped to catch his breath.

"Hey, Morgan," he called out. "Can I ask you something?"

McFulty stopped and turned toward him. "What?"

"Why is the air so heavy here? I didn't feel this when I was approaching the town."

McFulty tensed and his face started turning red. "You can feel the air because you're not like us."

"What does that mean?" Arnold asked.

McFulty let out a sigh. "You like to ask a lot of questions, don't you?"

Arnold nodded.

"Let's save that one for later," McFulty suggested.

Arnold caught his breath and they kept walking. Ahead there were large intertwined pipes. They leaked and dripped, barely held together with tape and plastic wrap.

"Is this your irrigation system?" Arnold asked.

"No. These pipes bring water to the top of the wheels."

"There's water in the wheels?"

"These things are the pride 'n' joy of this town, each more cherished than the last. When you ride one of those things, you get transported to a special place, somewhere you may never reach in your entire life. That's why there's always such a long wait to hop on. One ride is never enough when you can experience something like that." He tapped on one of the pipes. "This water powers a machine inside each dome that makes it all possible."

Arnold thought again about those nights at his hometown carnival. As far as he knew, the Ferris wheel he had looked at every summer was the same special place McFulty spoke of. Somewhere Arnold may never reach in his entire life, interlocking fingers with the girl next to him as he looked down below at the world, free from any more doubt.

"That sounds too good to be true," Arnold said, his eyes wide.

"It's hard to explain. It's something you have to experience for yourself. Wish you could though, really do."

Again there was an insincerity in McFulty's voice that Arnold tried to wrap his head around. It was still unclear if McFulty was guiding him out of danger or if he was leading him right into it. But Arnold continued to trust him, and followed him regardless, their footsteps, and McFulty's puffing breath, echoing in the dark tunnel.

McFulty pulled the window curtain to the side and scanned the street in front of his home. It was empty. He shuffled through the house and outside into his backyard. The air weighed down on him.

"There's still time," McFulty said to himself, and looked over at the bushes lining the side of his yard. He waved at them.

The bushes rustled. Arnold emerged from behind them and dashed toward the door, keeping his head low. He ran past McFulty and into the tent house. Just as quickly, McFulty used a number of complicated knots to tie the door shut at both sides.

"Hang on a sec. I'll get the lights."

Arnold felt around in the darkness, walking carefully, his arms stretched out. He grazed past a plush table that came up to his hip and extended all the way to the floor. He bent down and sat beside it, listening to McFulty struggle to move around in the dark.

"Here it is," McFulty said from the front of the house.

Light.

It took a second for Arnold's eyes to adjust. When they did, he looked up at the table he was leaning against to discover it wasn't a table at all but a couch, almost twice as large as a normal couch. The rest of the furniture was the same way: the coffee table, the television stand, the floor lamp in the corner by the windows.

"Everything is so . . . big," Arnold pointed out.

"You're right. Does that surprise you?" McFulty snapped back, almost insulted.

"A little. I knew there were big people in this town, but I guess I didn't expect big furniture too."

McFulty let out a pompous grunt. "We take a lot of pride in how things are here, myself included. We're big people with even bigger lives. And if anybody should come by and try to impose their ways on us, I'll tell you, it won't end well."

"Is that why I'm in all this danger? Because of my size?" Arnold asked.

McFulty gave Arnold a look, as if he were telling Arnold the obvious.

"But if that's true, why does it feel like everyone is ignoring me?"

"They can't see you," McFulty said.

"They can't see me?"

McFulty lumbered into the kitchen and opened the refrigerator—which was again bigger than any that Arnold had ever seen—and pulled out a half-carved ham that sat on a cutting board. Arnold walked toward the kitchen but then stopped, standing in the doorway.

"Do you realize that you're the first of your kind to step foot in this town in years?" McFulty asked.

"No."

"Well, it's true. How did you find this place?"

"Just by traveling."

McFulty whipped out a large blade from a drawer next to the sink and pressed it up against the skin of the ham. He struggled with it for a few seconds before producing a thick slice with jagged edges. He folded it into quarters and started eating it in big bites.

"Just by traveling? Where are you traveling to?"

"North," Arnold replied, keeping an eye on the blade.

"How far north?" McFulty carved off another uneven slice and folded it into his mouth.

"I haven't figured that out yet."

McFulty took the remaining ham and covered it in plastic wrap, placing it back inside the refrigerator. He shut the door.

"Well, you need to figure that out quick. 'Cause come tomorrow morning, you're out of here."

McFulty slipped past Arnold. His ham breath hovered over Arnold's face, penetrating his nostrils, and he could almost taste the meat on his tongue.

"Won't you tell me why, or what's going on?" Arnold asked.

"I can't do that!" McFulty exclaimed, pointing a finger to the ceiling.

The sound of tearing fabric pierced the air and they looked at each other awkwardly. Arnold peered under McFulty's armpit, where the tearing sound had come from, and saw a tuft of white cotton poking out. McFulty stepped back, looking down at the tear. He pulled at it as more cotton came out. He quickly placed his arm at his side and scurried toward his bedroom, closing the door behind him.

McFulty's muffled voice came from behind the door. "There's no time for this now, Arnold. I have to return to my shop before people notice I'm missing."

Arnold followed behind and pressed his ear up against the bedroom door, which was an actual door, and heard a loud rustling coming from the other side. McFulty seemed to be struggling with something.

"So what do you want me to do?" Arnold asked.

"Just . . . just wait here, Arnold. You have to stay here until I get back. Don't go anywhere."

McFulty remained in his bedroom for a while longer, and eventually Arnold walked back to the living room to sit on the couch and wait for him. When McFulty came out, he had on a new pair of overalls and his beard had been combed.

"I'll come back for you in a couple of hours, after my stand closes. I'm sorry, but this is just how it has to be. Come tomorrow, you need to be on your way north again. There's nothing for you here but a night's rest. That much I can offer."

Arnold wanted to speak up but said nothing. McFulty made for the front door flap and untied the knots, slipping through the opening. Once outside, he tied them together again. Arnold made for the window and peeked through, waiting until McFulty was down the block and out of sight. As soon as the last of him disappeared behind a house, Arnold headed toward the back door. With his small size, he was able to slip through without untying any knots.

Outside, the heavy air took a toll on him immediately, but he tried his best to fight through it. He wasn't going to wait for McFulty to come back or stay longer than he had to. He would find his way to the Tower and leave the town before anyone else could find him.

He circled the house and quietly snuck across the front lawn. On the other side of the street Arnold saw a forest and headed toward it, disappearing into the trees.

For a moment, he wanted to emerge from the other side of the forest and into his backyard at home. He would jump the creek and land on the flat rock planted firmly into the soil, near the spot where the mud had taken his shoe years ago. Then the last line of the trees would give way to the open grass and he'd sprint to the front of his house, landing on the porch steps. His father would pull into the driveway moments after; while inside, his mother's pot of boiling pasta would overflow. The neglected pot of water would spill onto the stove and the fire would shriek and lash out until the water evaporated. And he'd be home.

Instead he entered a twisted forest of tall trees funneling him forward, with no end in sight. By the time he stopped to catch his breath, he could barely see the sky past the lush foliage. The shrill of insects and the cooing of a distant bird penetrated his ears. The landscape had transformed. This was a place no one went to anymore. The shrubbery was unkempt and wild; twisting vines hugged thick branches, and wide tree trunks rooted a dozen feet underground.

He continued to catch his breath as sweet saliva built up along his jaw. He spit out a golf ball–sized glob of spittle onto the ground and walked forward, hands on his hips. The thick brush opened up into a clearing where he could see between the trees. The gray clouds had dispersed a bit, and blue sky was beginning to poke through. Then he saw it. Some sixty yards out, he saw the top of a great wheel, rusted red in color and much smaller than the rest in town. The peculiar hue intrigued him, and he decided to get a closer look.

The overgrowth around the great wheel was rampant. Thick, tangled vines devoured it almost all the way to the top, like the earth had risen from below and tried to swallow it whole.

Arnold stepped cautiously over patches of wild grass, approaching the great wheel as if it were a slumbering beast. He circled it twice until he found a spot with the least amount of vegetation to begin his climb. He wouldn't need to climb to the top—just high enough to peer over the trees and look for the Tower.

He grabbed handfuls of vines with each step. The wheel buckled at points where his weight was too heavy, but he secured himself by grabbing one of the exposed middle spokes. He was already halfway to the top, about five carts up, and he shinnied to the side along the middle spoke, toward one of the carts. He put his hands on the edge of the cart and pushed himself up, wrapping his arm around the drive rim for leverage. Gently, he eased himself inside. It creaked with each step, as if the wheel had awoken from a deep sleep. There was a shallow pool of brown water where the floor was creased with rotting leaves. On the inside of the cart, a metal plate hung loosely by one screw. It read:

LET THOSE WHOSE BRAVERY TO START ANEW BEGIN FROM THIS HIGH VIEW

The loose screw tempted him to finish the job that time had started.

He looked above the trees. In the distance, dozens of the massive wheels dotted the horizon. He ran his eyes down the tree line until he spotted a great wheel off to the side, alone. He recognized it slightly, thinking it might be the one he'd seen when he'd first arrived. The Tower was there somewhere, and getting back to it wasn't going to be easy.

In this foreign place, he was beginning to worry about the Tower.

He wiped leaves and dirt off the cart bench and sat down, staring at the metal plate. His mind wandered once more to those summer nights in his hometown. He looked to his right, where the seat of the imaginary girls from past summers was empty. He rested his hand on the bench and opened his palm.

This must be that special place, he thought as he clenched his fist.

Under the shroud of the forest, it got darker much faster and Arnold was growing tired from wandering. He was lost. The forest never gave way to another clearing, and he had no idea which direction to go in to find the great wheel he had seen above the tree line. Eventually he navigated his way back to the rusted wheel and began climbing it again to regain his bearings.

He boosted himself up onto one of the carts and grabbed a handful of vines, stretching toward the exposed middle spoke. He lifted himself onto it and reached for the cart above him, pushing down onto the spoke and leaping for the next cart. He gripped the edge of it, but his fingers slipped and he fell back down onto the middle spoke. Suddenly, the wheel creaked and the spoke gave way. Arnold fell backward and came crashing down onto the ground as the carts became unhinged and fell on top of one another. He scurried on his hands and knees and nearly missed being crushed as the carts tipped and slammed into the ground. Arnold caught his breath and got to his feet as particles of rust hung in the air over the wreckage. He wiped leaves from his clothes and coughed, trying to clear the air with his hand.

It was getting late, and he realized that he had no choice but to go along with McFulty's plan. He headed back toward where he had entered the forest.

Maybe he'll help me find the Tower, he thought.

The trees started to dissipate and Arnold emerged back onto the field across the street from McFulty's home. He ran toward it, keeping an eye out for anyone who might be close by. He approached the front lawn and circled around to the back, passing by a window on the side of the house. There was a noise coming from inside, more rustling and groaning, similar to what he'd heard before, after McFulty's shirt had torn.

Arnold approached the window and peeked inside, between the slit of the knotted cloth.

He froze. A dark figure stood in the middle of the hall. McFulty's face was on another man's body, and the man was holding a large sack. Arnold screamed and fell backward. The slim, lanky figure wearing McFulty's face shrieked and held his hands out.

"No, wait. This isn't what it looks like!" the slim man yelled.

Arnold stumbled to his feet and dashed toward the front of the house. The man called out to him as he wrestled with the sack.

"Arnold, stop! You can't be outside!" he pleaded.

Arnold ignored the man's words and started to run, panting almost instantly from the heavy air. But he fought through it, running until his heart banged against his chest, taking a hammer to his rib cage.

After navigating the streets and backyards of tent homes, he was far enough from McFulty's that he felt like he could stop. The sun was setting, and the sky was a brilliant hue of pink and purple. He took a moment to breathe deeply as the air around him finally seemed to weigh less. The sounds of the festival had quieted down substantially too, and he listened carefully for any noise that would alert him to someone's presence.

Arnold turned into a large open field and followed a path through concrete benches and dilapidated columns circling a stone slab where a building used to stand. He picked up his pace to a light jog, moving toward a fence bordering the backyard of another home. He slipped past a tall concrete structure, sticking close to it as he got nearer to the fence.

Just as he cleared the concrete structure, he caught a glimpse of a pair of bright blue eyes and round red cheeks staring back at him. Huddled around one of the concrete benches was a family that now had an unobstructed view of Arnold. A mother, father, and two girls, each one more plump than the next. The blue-eyed girl shrieked at the sight of Arnold.

"Mommy, Mommy! It's a thinny!" she called out.

Her voice startled him and Arnold took off, knowing well enough he could outrun them and their lumbering bodies. The mother and father hobbled to their feet and called for him to stop. Arnold ignored them and ran straight for the fence and jumped over it, sprinting toward the street. He ran to the end of the block and checked behind him. The family was nowhere to be found.

"Too slow," he said with a chuckle.

76

He turned his head forward again and ran smack into a large body that bounced him backward onto the pavement. He shook his head and looked up at the smug face towering over him. A beast of a man stared at Arnold, his lip curled both in shock and in anger.

"Now, now, look at this thinny right here!" the man exclaimed.

Arnold continued to look up, at a loss for words. He raised his hand, as if to reason with the man. A crowd began to form around the two of them, and in no time he was surrounded.

"Well, say somethin', thinny," the man spoke again. He was still standing over Arnold, his large body blocking out the setting sun.

"I don't mean any trouble. I was just about to leave."

"Call me a thickbelly, boy, I dare you," the man said. "Say it!"

"I don't mean any trouble," Arnold repeated.

He looked at the crowd, who were equally angered by his presence. His mind raced at the dwindling possibilities of escape. Then, through the sea of people, he saw him: McFulty, head and body now intact, looking on with concerned eyes.

"I—" Arnold began.

"Jessie!" McFulty interrupted Arnold, calling to the beast.

The beast, Jessie, turned around as the crowd slowly scuttled backward to make room for him. Through Jessie's legs Arnold saw McFulty at the front of the crowd.

"What are you doing?" McFulty asked.

"Morgan, just in time. We're gonna tear this thinny in two for steppin' onto our land. You can have at 'im next."

McFulty made his way to Arnold and stood next to him.

"Don't lay a hand on him, Jessie."

There was a murmur in the crowd. Jessie looked at McFulty as if it were the first time anyone had told him no.

"Excuse me?" Jessie exclaimed. "You've lost your marbles, old man, if you think I'm gonna let this thinny just walk on outta here."

"What's it gonna solve, Jessie? What's one thinny gonna do to us?" McFulty pleaded.

"It always starts with one!" a voice called out from the crowd. "More will come."

A volley of *yeahs* and nods of agreement peppered the crowd.

"You know that, Morgan. What's one thinny to you?" Jessie asked, rubbing his knuckles against the palm of his other hand.

McFulty looked down at Arnold with a gaze he had seen before. He recognized it from his father. There was sadness and a deep burden to implicate himself for something that had gotten out of hand. Arnold knew the look well, and McFulty wore it like a pro.

"I won't let you hurt him, Jessie," McFulty continued, his eyes closed. "He's my son."

There were gasps from the crowd and McFulty bent down to help Arnold to his feet, dusting his shoulders off.

"What?" Jessie bellowed. "Your son?"

"I've been keeping him a secret for far too long," McFulty announced to the crowd. "But now it's time for me to come clean."

"Why does he look like that? What's wrong with 'im?" asked someone from the crowd.

"It's a . . . disease. It's out of his control. Believe me . . . if I could change him, I would," McFulty declared to the onlooking faces, and pulled Arnold in closer. "So, what's it gonna be, Jessie?"

Jessie looked out to the crowd for reassurance.

"We got rules here, Morgan. And you been hiding this from us all this time . . . ," Jessie began, then let out a long sigh. "But I got respect for you."

McFulty smirked and gave Arnold a nod.

"So I'm gonna give you till tomorrow's sunset for both of y'all to leave town. Leave and never come back."

"No, wait! I'll go," Arnold interjected. "I'll go and Morgan can stay."

"It ain't up to you, thinny. We're all in agreement here," Jessie said confidently as he looked at the crowd.

Then Arnold looked out at the crowd too, noticing the sternness of all the faces staring back at him, with crossed arms and clenched fists. Not one person, aside from McFulty, thought differently on the matter. Jessie pulled back and made for the edge of the crowd as it began to disperse.

"Consider yourself lucky that I'm goin' easy on you," Jessie said with his back turned to Arnold and McFulty. "Sunset. Tomorrow. And we'll be there to make sure you're gone."

The street cleared out and Arnold felt like he was finally able to breathe again. He looked at McFulty, who was busy staring at the ground, wiping tears from his eyes. He sniffled and looked at Arnold. His puffy eyes exaggerated the crow's-feet clawing at his skin.

"I'm sorry," Arnold whispered.

They made it only a couple of blocks before McFulty had to stop. He sat down on the curb and looked out at the sunset. Arnold sat beside him. They hadn't spoken since McFulty had been banished by the people who had just earlier that day revered him.

"I'm sorry for getting you in trouble," Arnold said, his voice like a jagged knife cutting the silence. "But you scared me pretty bad back there."

"I know," he said. "It's my fault. I shouldn't have reacted the way I did. I just . . . It's been a long time comin', Arnold." McFulty stroked his long gray beard and continued to stare at the sky, his eyes red and veiny.

Their shadows grew taller as time slipped away. Arnold hung his head, looking down at the ground between his legs. He let his eyes glaze over and lose focus while the wind blew at his hair and fluttered over his eyelashes.

His eyes refocused and he took notice of a coin on the ground; it had a face that stared back at him. He wondered where it came from and how it ended up on the street, invisible to everyone but him.

He pictured a hungry man buying a chocolate bar. In his pocket he jingled the loose change he would use to buy it. After the purchase, he walked home eating the candy, throwing the wrapper and the receipt onto the sidewalk. And as he threw the receipt away, a stray coin was stuck inside the crumpled paper. It hit the concrete without the man noticing. Then time and nature took a turn, freeing the coin from captivity until it ended up in the very spot next to where Arnold sat.

He thought about the value of the coin and how it only had any when it was in someone's hands. On its own, it was powerless. Its fate was determined by when the winds decided to move or when someone cared enough to pick it up again. Ultimately, the potential of the coin was not its own to decide.

Arnold looked over at McFulty, who was still gazing out at the sky, and then turned away to hide his eyes.

McFulty agreed to help Arnold find his way back to the Tower.

"I have to get something that I left behind," Arnold had said when McFulty urged them to go home.

The time apart had felt like an eternity to Arnold, but the Tower was intact, just the way he had left it. He had the festival to thank for that, and the very idea made him chuckle. He gave the Tower a nod and then began checking it.

"What in the world is this?" McFulty exclaimed, suddenly injected with life.

"This is . . . my travel companion," Arnold said, still unsure of what to call it.

"That's no companion," McFulty said. "It's more like a walking attention grabber. I'm glad you had the wherewithal to hide it."

"I didn't have much of a choice," said Arnold. "The air was so heavy at the time, I could barely walk."

"Oh yeah, it's been so long, I stopped paying attention to that," McFulty said as he turned his body to the street. "The air gets that way during the festival, side effect of the pheromones produced from the wheels."

"Pheromones?"

"Remember when I told you that nobody could see you?" McFulty asked, turning back to Arnold.

"Yes."

"Well, that's why," McFulty continued. "At the cost of giving up their security for a day, the people here allow themselves to be put into a trance from the exhaust of the wheels. It clouds their minds, makes the air heavier, and keeps them in a state of bliss."

"Why would they do that when they're so careful about who comes into town?" Arnold asked.

"It's a risk they're willing to take. Nobody like you has ever had the unfortunate coincidence of stumbling upon this place during the festival."

Arnold stroked his chin.

"Then how did you see me?"

McFulty walked closer to the Tower and stood in its shadow, looking up at the enormous structure. "How about we get back to my home first before anything else happens?"

Arnold narrowed his eyes at McFulty before complying with an "Okay," then pushed back the Tower's kickstand. Even with the heavier air, pushing the cart across town was the easiest thing he'd done all day.

Inside McFulty's home, Arnold hopped up onto the living room couch and sat down as McFulty leaned back on a recliner in the corner near the floor lamp. The big man let out a long sigh, removing his hat and running his hands through his thinning gray hair.

"You remind me of a long-gone time, Arnold . . . ," he began. "A time when I didn't go by the name Morgan McFulty."

"When was that?"

"A time when I looked like you," McFulty continued. "In public, anyways."

"What do you mean?"

McFulty stood up, staring at Arnold without blinking. He placed his hands at the back of his neck and pulled at a string underneath his collar, lifting it above his head and down the side of his body. It released a zipper that he then pulled down all the way to the small of his back. His hands disappeared through the sleeves of his shirt, one after the other, and his belly, his soft, round, thick belly, slid down his legs and to his ankles.

A new man stood before Arnold, one resembling the man he had caught a glimpse of through the window, earlier that day. But now it was McFulty, a tall, lanky man covered in a gray one-piece from the neck down, like a great moth that had regressed into a larva.

"This is the real me," McFulty said.

Arnold sat back on the couch. "You're hiding yourself. Why?"

McFulty let out a sharp sigh and sat back down in his chair, which was now comically larger than he was.

"I had a son. . . ." he said. "He was about your age. Loved to read and stare out at the sky on clear nights. Of course, where we lived, you could barely make out the moon, there were so many lights. But still, he'd climb the fire escape on weekends and just lie there. I'd bring him sandwiches and we would stargaze together. Just the two of us. Boy, he loved a good sandwich. Anything with mustard, that was his favorite. The boy could eat a whole jar in one sitting.

"But our city wasn't as simple as that. A failing economy triggered shortages in food supplies and the people started to turn on one another, casting blame on big people. It reached a boiling point, spreading to my office, to my block, to my front door. Things quickly got violent. A lot of people ran away, my son and I included.

"The citizens who were pushed out staked their claim here, all of 'em much like the people before you today—a strong people who would develop a deep-rooted hatred for anyone not like them. So we had to blend in."

McFulty paused to gather himself. "About three months later, he got sick."

He got up from the recliner and looked out the window, into the dark suburban street.

"My son, he . . . It wasn't something this place was prepared to deal with. He had a virus, somethin' that ate him from the inside. It became harder and harder to conceal him as he kept dropping weight, and I was too afraid to expose us, afraid we might be sent back to our city . . . or worse."

He turned to face Arnold. "I've been hiding ever since, alone."

Arnold remained still on the couch. Then he finally spoke. "They wouldn't help you?"

"This town swore off people like you and me, even threatening to kill any who crossed town lines. There was no one I could turn to."

McFulty bent down and picked up his suit, folding it into a ball in his arms.

"I need to start packing before it gets light out," he said, letting the folded-up suit hang loosely. "You can stay the night. There's an extra bed down the hall you can use."

"You're not really going to leave, are you?" asked Arnold. "These people wouldn't help you when you needed them most. You don't owe them anything."

"What do you propose I do then, Arnold? Ask them to stay? Get on my hands and knees and beg?"

Arnold folded his arms and looked away from McFulty.

"I'm done hiding, Arnold. I should've been done a long time ago."

Arnold stared at a brown water spot on the ceiling above him in his larger-than-average bed. Down the hall, he could hear McFulty rummaging through his drawers, filling suitcases with clothes he would never wear again. Despite McFulty's insistence that leaving was inevitable, he couldn't help but feel guilty for everything that had happened. He felt restless.

He got up and looked out the window. The Tower stood just outside, blocking part of his view of the backyard. He had a sudden, strange sensation that he would sleep better if he crawled up into the perch in the Tower, but he knew it wasn't big enough to accommodate a full night's rest.

Finally he left his room and tiptoed to McFulty's. The door was wide open this time.

"Can't sleep?" McFulty asked, flanked by large, bulging black bags tied at the tops.

Arnold shook his head.

"Well, if you can't sleep, might as well help."

He tossed Arnold a large roll of unused black bags. Arnold smirked and opened one up. McFulty pointed to a pile of corduroy pants near his dresser.

"Start there. Might be easier to get 'em all in if you fold 'em," he suggested.

"Okay." Arnold grabbed a pair of green pants and started folding them on the floor.

"So, why don't you tell me about that thing you've got parked outside?" McFulty asked.

"What do you want to know?"

"Well, for starters . . . maybe what it is?" McFulty asked.

Arnold fished for words as he gently folded the pair of green pants and placed them in the bag.

"It's home . . . ," Arnold began. "Or . . . that's what it used to be."

"How is that home?"

"It's everything I took from home when I ran away. My clothes, my parents' clothes, everything—right down to the silverware. Now it's mine to carry until I can find a new place to call home."

McFulty slowed his packing to a crawl. "It must've taken a lot of courage to do that."

"I'm not so sure," Arnold replied. "It was more than just courage. It was a lot of . . . anger, too."

McFulty seemed to be deep in thought. "What're you lookin' for?" he asked.

"I don't know."

"Are you waitin' for somethin'?"

"No."

"Runnin' from somethin'?"

Arnold went silent and placed another folded pair of pants in the black bag. McFulty let out a long sigh and stroked his beard, looking up at the ceiling.

"I'm not running from something," Arnold said finally. "I'm just looking for something . . . better."

McFulty continued to stroke his beard. Arnold continued placing clothes inside the black bag. After a long pause, McFulty spoke.

"There's a place called Kingdom."

"Kingdom?"

"It's a faraway place, as far east as you can possibly go."

"What's there?"

"Oh, I've never been, but I've heard the stories. Utopia. Sanctuary. Oasis . . . Graveyard . . . Mirage . . . Those are just some of the words whispered by people who know about it. Others claim it's a feeling, something beyond words or understanding. There's no real way of knowing, 'cause all who've dared to journey there've never returned."

"Why haven't they returned?"

"I don't know," McFulty admitted. "But the stories find their way around the world somehow. Maybe for you, it's a place you can call home—the 'better' you're looking for."

"It doesn't sound like there's any guarantee it's even a good place."

"You're right."

Arnold looked around the room, thinking.

"But you could make it," McFulty said. "Especially with that thing you got outside."

"What do you mean?"

"It's a long journey east and you'll need supplies. You've got everything you need out there to do it."

"If it's so great, why haven't you gone?"

"I'm an old man, Arnold," McFulty replied, shaking his head. "I could never make a journey like that. Besides, there's no 'better' without my son."

"I'm sorry. I didn't mean—"

"Kingdom may be a special place, but that's no replacement for family. Home is not a home without family. Wherever you decide to go from here, whether you search for Kingdom or continue on the path you're on, that's something you should also carry with you. Take it from an old man."

Arnold went back to filling the bag with McFulty's clothes, keeping his head down. The rest of the evening was filled with the rustling of black plastic bags. As the last few stars in the sky revealed themselves, Arnold went back to bed, his mind heavier than ever.

The next morning, Arnold woke up earlier than he'd anticipated. He hadn't slept much. He poked his head out of the bedroom. It was silent in the house, but he heard a faint snoring coming from McFulty's room. He stepped through the back door and walked toward the Tower.

It slept, hidden under cover of a tree along the side of the house. A light morning dew coated it. Arnold removed his long-sleeve shirt and began wiping down the cart. He hung the damp shirt on a piece of metal poking out from the side of the Tower, and stepped up onto the plank. He wasn't exactly sure what he was looking for, but he began sifting through the Tower's contents anyway. Without knowing the layout of the pieces of the Tower, it was a game of chance to find anything specific.

He climbed up into the perch. Inside, he saw the toolbox, but he wasn't concerned with that now. He scanned the walls, looking for a sign, something he could give to McFulty as an apology. He turned his body so the light could illuminate the hole. Suddenly he felt a sharp pain in his arm and pulled it back.

There was a long scratch there now, and it began to bleed. A sharp blade was poking out of the Tower. He carefully dug his fingers around the blade, revealing a long orange handle, and pulled it out. He held it against the sunlight and began to examine it. Then it hit him.

An hour later, the back door rustled open. McFulty, the fat one, stood there sipping on something in a large brown mug. Arnold could see the steam coming off it, and the smell wafted toward him. Hot chocolate.

"You're up early," McFulty called out to him.

Arnold hopped down onto the plank as McFulty took notice of a dozen knives that were laid out in front of the Tower. With a new purpose for each knife, they were easier for Arnold to give away. He felt like, at least for McFulty's help, that the Tower understood and accepted its release.

"I know it's not much," Arnold said. "And this probably doesn't make up for anything, but wherever you end up next, you're going to need a better set of knives to make those sandwiches."

McFulty looked over the array of knives and then up at Arnold.

"You know, under different circumstances, I'd be pretty scared to see a bunch o' blades on my lawn."

A smile crept onto McFulty's face and Arnold took notice of all his wrinkles stacking on top of one another. They told a story that words couldn't. McFulty bent down to look at a butcher's blade and then ran his finger along the handle.

"Thank you for this, Arnold," he said, looking him in the eyes.

Arnold nodded and smiled at him as the sun splashed McFulty's face. McFulty was a mix of emotions: hopelessness, sadness, relief. Arnold was filled with some of the same feelings, and he had to look away from the old man again.

"What about the rest of it?" McFulty asked as he got closer, giving the Tower a once-over. "Have you decided what you're going to do yet?"

"I thought about what you said, about Kingdom," Arnold said. "I could keep going north and find whatever's in that direction, or I could go east. But how can I be sure it isn't anything but a pipe dream? You've never been there, and you said the people who do go there never return."

"You're right: there's nothing I can really give to you as proof," McFulty admitted. "You know about as much as I do now. All I offer is an option."

Arnold leaned back against the Tower and folded his arms, looking down at his feet.

"Why are you doing this?"

"Doing what?"

"Helping me."

"It's too late for me and my son . . . but I can still do some good here," McFulty said, folding his arms to match Arnold. "As someone who's also run away from home . . . I don't want your journey to be for nothin' too.

"Whatever it is, whatever I've heard about what it is . . . You could be happy there."

Arnold glanced back up. "I'll think about it."

McFulty nodded at him and offered up another smile. Arnold thought about his journey thus far and the uncertainty he felt on a daily basis. He pondered the idea that a tangible goal, a place he could reach and be happy, would help him keep going and suppress the constant doubts that plagued his mind. He thought about the chance encounter of meeting McFulty, someone just like him, living among people who weren't like him, trying his best to get by. He wondered, if there was ever a sign he should follow, if this was it.

Later that morning, Arnold and the Tower left the town before McFulty did, ensuring that if Jessie or anyone else came to him, he wouldn't be there to add more fuel to the already raging fire. As the great wheels of the town began to shrink, Arnold indulged in the thought that McFulty would return to his home, ready to pick up the pieces of his past, and start over.

Outside the town, Arnold paused, pushing the Tower's brake into the ground. Then he stood looking out at the horizon, his arms at his sides. Ahead was home. Behind him, the path north he had been following for days. And to his left, somewhere out past sand dunes, thick forests, and mountains whose names he would never know, lay Kingdom, a place shrouded in nothing but a haze of hope. The thought tempted him, but at the same time, a lingering doubt pulled him back in the direction of home. In just a week's hike, he could take it all back and pretend this was nothing more than a dream. All it would take was a heartfelt apology, a commitment to rebuilding their home, and an oath to make amends with the family, to stick by them until he became old and gray, like McFulty.

He looked at the Tower, his ticket to Kingdom.

"Do you think it's harder to be true to yourself or to be true to someone else?" Arnold asked the Tower. There was silence, and Arnold nodded in agreement.

He looked to his left again and then down at his compass. East.

East, toward the place called Kingdom. A place he could call home. A place for him and the Tower. It was too much of a coincidence to ignore, that the Tower, the thing he had created out of spite, could now be his greatest salvation.

There was no way to be sure, but it was a direction. The great wheels were now an afterthought in the distance, and Arnold was as far and as close to Kingdom as he had ever been.

4

STOPGAP

It was during the fourth week of traveling east that Arnold started paying more attention to the sky. More specifically, the sun. Every morning when the sun rose, he was woken up by its light, and it seemed to get brighter and brighter with each passing day. Just as he had gotten used to his compass guiding him east, he now had the increasingly white sky to follow instead.

In the last few days, the terrain had become flat and dry, with dust and debris frequently kicking up into his eyes. An incessant squeaking in the front right wheel nagged him. He stopped to fix it, going as far as nearly disassembling the entire wheel, but stopped when he feared that he would ruin the tire for good. So he tried his best to tune out the squeaking.

It all paled in comparison to the great white light that filled the sky the farther east he traveled.

Arnold stopped the Tower in its tracks and shoved the kickstand into the dirt. The ground was tough, so he sat on the plank to add more weight and press the two brakes in farther. The dirt attacking his eyes coupled with the sun's brightness meant it was time to take a break.

Facing west, he could see the sun's rays flaring out from the sides of the Tower. It cast a shadow over him. As bright as the sun was, it wasn't any warmer outside: rather, it was quite the opposite.

He stood up and climbed up into the perch. Over the past four weeks, he had used a hammer from the toolbox to widen the space and make more room for the things he used often— the toolbox, a small toiletry bag he'd found, some sweaters and a blanket for cold nights, among other things. This time, he reached for a burgundy zip-up sweater and his sunglasses and put them on.

He hopped down. There were a lot of things poking out of the Tower. At the front, near where part of the tarp stuck out, there was a half-revealed black trash bag. He thought about poking a hole into the bag to search its insides, but he was afraid the Tower might shift and collapse in on itself.

He turned again toward the sun, shielding his eyes with his hand, and let out a sigh of frustration. The sunglasses did little to protect his vision.

"I guess I'll just wait it out," he said to the Tower.

He knew in doing so he'd lose most of the day, but it was better than being constantly blinded by light and dust. Arnold gave the tarp a good tug—to his surprise it slid out a bit. This caught him off guard, and he quickly pulled at the tarp again. This time, it didn't budge. Opportunity had briefly met chance and given him a second of luck.

He circled around the back and lay down on the plank, staring up at the sky. Sparks fired in his eyes and danced across the blue plain. It was just him and the Tower. Its shadow hugged every corner of Arnold's body and lulled him to sleep, watching over him while he lay there and began to drift off. He felt safer now than he had in a long time, next to his watchful giant of memories.

Arnold had a dream. He was lying in his bed back home. The house was empty. He looked out his bedroom window into the street. The night before, an unusual storm had hit his town. It knocked down trees and power lines and flooded the streets, leaving his home without electricity. After realizing he was alone and nothing in his house worked, he went for a walk to get a closer look at all the damage.

As he walked down the street, he noticed that other homes were still lit up, as if nothing had happened the day before, as if the damage had affected only his house. Windows shone bright yellow, and streetlights illuminated the overcast neighborhood. Arnold circled the block to find more of the same, then headed back to his house to see the lights were still off.

He got closer and noticed the large tree in his backyard was missing. He walked over to see that it had fallen over during the storm, barely missing his house. It was a massive tree, stripped of most its branches from the ferocious winds. The ground surrounding it was littered with remains: leaves, twigs, bark, and hundreds of acorns. He maneuvered past the twisting debris to get closer, and that was when he saw it. Amid the carnage of tattered limbs was a lone acorn, still dangling from its branch. Arnold looked around. Among a sea of fallen, one had survived.

He reached out to touch it, but just as he was about to, he heard a thunderous *crack*. He jerked his head up just as the giant tree in Mr. Wu's backyard snapped at its base and came toppling over him, crashing down with immense force. And then he woke up.

Arnold flung his eyes open as water dripped from above. The sky was swollen with black clouds.

He sprang to his feet and looked at the Tower as raindrops started to accumulate. It was unprotected. He rushed to the opposite side, where the tarp still poked out. His only choice now was to free the tarp from captivity or suffer through the Tower's imminent drowning.

Arnold locked onto the bright yellow tarp staring back at him, grabbed a fistful of it in each hand, and pulled. The bones in his arms stiffened and every muscle bulged. His arms shook.

He gritted his teeth. He anchored his feet into the fresh mud and dug deeper with each pull.

Again.

And again.

And again.

Each pull was harder than the last. Arnold turned around and flipped his grip, yanking the tarp over his shoulder. With each step, he sunk deeper into the muck. He was amazed at how quickly the ground had become soft. The Tower creaked and the kickstand buckled. Water dripped down his forehead and into his mouth.

Thunder cracked above him. A fierce storm was forming.

The thunder cracked again, startling him into jumping forward. And as he did, the tarp sprang free. It fell on top of Arnold and he tumbled into the mud as a slew of bathroom toiletries flew out. The Tower shifted and hunched forward slightly.

Arnold frantically pulled the tarp off himself, splashing around in the sticky sludge. He spit some dirt out of his mouth and freed his head, looking out toward the east. His disgusting feeling was short-lived.

The bright light.

The sun.

Through the fog of the storm, it was still there. Despite hours of rest and the passing of time, the sun remained frozen in the east, infinitely rising and infinitely not. He was at a loss for words. Then it suddenly dawned on him.

"That's not the sun."

Arnold covered the Tower with the tarp. It was just big enough to wrap around the top, and it hung loosely above his head as he sat on the plank. The tarp was a newcomer in the ever-expanding rotation of items in his home. Now it protected him and the Tower from the elements.

Arnold huddled under the overhang of the Tower, waiting for the rain to stop. The light from the east continued to shine through the gray of the storm. He waited for what seemed like an eternity. Hours passed and the storm neither died down nor intensified, just as the light had neither increased nor decreased. He thought it might last forever, and his patience was wearing thin.

"I don't think this is going to pass," he said to the Tower.

Arnold zipped up his sweater and put up his hood, climbing out from under the Tower's protection. He slid the plank under the cart, lifted up the kickstand from the mud, and pushed the Tower toward the light, slicing it in two, keeping equal light on both sides to guide the Tower forward. The storm seemed to intensify with each step. It rained harder and the wind howled past his ears. It was as if the storm were trying to keep him away, but the resistance only motivated him more.

The light created a white wall in front of him that began to consume everything. Slowly, the Tower began to disappear until he couldn't see his own hand in front of his face. Completely blinded by light, he pushed harder, a lone soldier marching blindfolded into battle.

Then, as quickly as the storm had appeared, it disappeared. And as it did, so did the intensity of the light.

Arnold slipped and fell and his momentum pushed the Tower forward a bit. He coughed up some dust and got to his feet, removing his hood from his soaked hair. He rubbed his eyes. The white wall had disappeared, and in its place he saw something else: a city built into a tall white mountain range. He stood there, mystified. Looking up at the now-blue sky, he saw the sun, the real sun, and saw that it was in its correct place. And behind him was a wall of gray that seemed to be an illusion.

Arnold stretched his arm into the wall of gray and let out a chuckle of pure wonder.

"What the—"

He pulled his arm back—his hand was now dripping with water. He looked up. The wall of gray extended up into the sky.

He walked back to the Tower and peeled off his sweater, hanging it on the end of a broomstick poking out of the Tower's belly. Then, reluctantly, he took off his pants and hung them as well, slightly embarrassed at suddenly being so naked. He had been soaked to the skin.

He removed the tarp, folded it as best he could, and then placed it inside the perch. He climbed down and pushed the Tower along. With the mountain range being so wide, his shortest route was through it. He estimated it was at least an hourlong walk to the city, and he was okay with that. He hoped to be dry and wearing pants again by the time he got to the entrance. The important thing, he told himself, was that he was still heading east, toward Kingdom.

As he approached the base of the mountain, two long spires stood flanking the entry road up into the canyon. About one hundred yards away, Arnold begrudgingly squirmed back into his still-wet pants. The cold cotton suctioned onto his skin and sent shivers down his spine.

"You can leave them off!" a voice from above suddenly called out.

It came from one of the spires. He could barely make out the person from all the surrounding white, but whoever it was waved to him.

"Uhh . . . what?" Arnold responded.

"I said you can leave them off!" the voice called to him again.

Arnold looked around in confusion. "My pants?"

There were some whispers between the two spires. Another man was inside the second one.

"Yes!"

Arnold arched an eyebrow.

"No, wait . . . your shoes!" the voice called out again. "Please remove your shoes."

Arnold looked down at the caked-on mud on his soles.

"Your shoes!" the voice repeated.

"Why?" Arnold asked.

There was more whispering.

"You're not from here," the voice called out. "If you want to enter our city, we ask you to respect our wishes."

He looked down at his feet again and then back up at the spires, squinting. Then he removed his muddy shoes and placed them underneath the cart.

"Okay, you're free to enter!" the voice called out one more time before disappearing from the spire window.

Past the spires, Arnold stretched his toes out onto the warm sandstone of the road and rubbed his feet against it. It felt good. He stood there a little longer to warm up his cold feet, then grabbed the Tower and pushed it through the entrance, up into the canyon.

When he arrived, the white city overwhelmed him. The cobblestone roads that spiraled up and down hills, the bikes people rode between narrow streets, even the clothes they wore—they were all white. Everything, aside from the animals, like the birds that flew overhead or the cats that napped above shop doors, followed suit. It was like something out of a fairy tale he had never heard of. The city was pristine, and he understood now why he was asked to take off his shoes. Keeping a city white meant keeping the dirt out.

Arnold made his way down more narrow cobbled streets that rose and fell through the mountain. He looked around at the people dressed in white clothes draped down their backs or wrapped around their faces. Walking barefoot, in colored clothes, with the Tower, made him stick out more than he wanted to. He thought it would be a good idea to try to fit in, feeling a bit apprehensive after his experience at the town of great wheels. But a trio of travelers wearing colored clothing passed by, and their presence put him a little more at ease. He didn't feel the immediate need to hide, just to find a way to blend in as much as possible. Getting dressed in something white seemed like the best idea.

The city was quiet, filled mainly with the faint conversations of people inside restaurants and bars. He didn't mind it though. Arnold found calm in ambient noise. The whisper of a tree caught in the wind, the vibration of conversations across a plaza, the hum of some sort of engine or oven in a local shop— the white noise wrapped around Arnold and made him feel comfortable. It encouraged him to slow down and take his time.

He passed a street with an open market that stretched for blocks, lined with little shops that sold ceramics, clothing, spices, fruits, and many other things he couldn't see. He eyed a shop selling white clothing, but it was a ways down and there was no discernable way to get the Tower there without causing a scene.

A couple more tourists in colored clothing walked by.

He continued past the market, looking for a small side street, one where he could park the Tower just long enough to run to the shop and back.

But he had no luck. The best he could find was an alley that narrowed at a sharp angle. He thought about shoving the Tower into it, blocking foot traffic and deterring people for a couple of minutes. But it was a big risk, and it put the Tower in harm's way.

I can't abandon it, Arnold thought.

His irrational fear was that poachers or thieves would surround the Tower and steal everything if he wasn't near it. No Tower meant no Kingdom and the possibilities it held for him. He couldn't let that happen.

Finally he made his decision. He'd bring the Tower with him. It would be messy and probably draw more attention to him than he wanted, but it was better than leaving the Tower unattended.

He rolled the Tower back to the intersection of the street market and once more eyed the store that sold the white clothes. With a nervous breath, he turned the Tower in and started wheeling it through, peeking around the sides to make sure he didn't hit anything.

The Tower rolled over everything. The wheels sucked up rags that ripped with ease, knocked over vases and other ceramics, and caught the attention of clerks and customers alike. Arnold's face flushed a deep red and he started to sweat.

He made it about ten steps before stopping. A shopkeeper jumped from his seat and started yelling at him in a language he had never heard before.

"I'm sorry," Arnold pleaded to the man. "I'll pay you back for everything. I'm sorry."

Suddenly his grip on the cart came loose. The shopkeeper spun him around and squeezed his arm hard, and Arnold couldn't help but wince. The shopkeeper yelled incessantly, getting in his face while Arnold tried to decipher the words as best he could. He understood none of it, only the clerk's obvious and reasonable anger.

Arnold felt a crowd form around him. They closed in, some staring him down, others more interested in the fifteen-foot-tall structure that had just smashed their merchandise. Arnold kept one hand firmly on the cart as it continued to drift away from him.

He tried to rip his arm away from the shopkeeper but fell down in the process, with the shopkeeper falling as well. He lost a handle on the Tower, and it started to roll away from him. While he was pinned down, he watched the hands multiply as the Tower continued to drift.

"Hey, you get off him right now!" a voice called out.

There was a whacking noise and a scuffle above him. A woman, dressed from the neck down in an elegant white robe, a rolled newspaper in her hand, was swatting at the shopkeeper who had pinned Arnold down. A few feet away, a man, also wearing a robe from the neck down, shooed away the crowd that had formed around the Tower.

The shopkeeper rolled off him and turned his attention to the woman, yelling again in that language Arnold didn't understand. What he did understand was that the woman was holding her composure much better than the shopkeeper was. She had a certain pragmatic presence about her.

Arnold looked at the Tower. The man in the robe was now standing next to it, holding a ceramic cup in his hand. He was enjoying the drink as if nothing had happened. Arnold took a moment to look around as the crowd dissolved and people returned to the shops. He got to his feet and saw that the shopkeeper was walking away, muttering something that had to be curses.

"My, my, are you all right, darling?" a soft voice asked him. The woman placed her hand on Arnold's face and combed his hair behind his ear. He could do nothing but accept her affection. "You look terribly shaken."

She began dusting him off with her rolled-up newspaper, making a point not to get herself dirty in the process. "These people can be quite savage sometimes. You would think they were selling the finest wares in the city." She then called out to the man, "Are you all right, darling?"

"Yes, of course, my love. Just a scuff here and there per-haps," he said.

"I hope those savages didn't spill your tea."

"Not a chance," the man said as he took a sip. He turned his attention to Arnold. "Young man, I believe this"—he looked at the Tower—"belongs to you. And while I would not mind returning it, I would not feel comfortable touching it without your permission. However, I will remain here until you are able to retrieve it."

Arnold noticed that the man accentuated the *h*'s in his speech.

He walked over to the Tower and did a quick survey of it. It seemed okay.

"Thank you," Arnold said to the man.

"You should be more careful," the woman insisted. "What would compel a young man such as yourself to cause such a ruckus?"

"I was looking to buy one of those white robes so I could fit in a little better."

Their faces lit up.

"Such a smart young man," the woman said. "What is your name?"

"Arnold."

"Arnold, you wait right here while I go fetch you one."

"Oh no, that's fine. I can just get one. . . ."

But the woman was already halfway to the shop.

"Relax, son," the man said. "Let's get this thing of yours out of the street before these hooligans cause another scene."

Together, Arnold and the man wheeled the Tower backward out of the street, moving carefully so as not to hit anything else. Every merchant was giving Arnold a look of death. He felt ashamed for his poor decision. The woman returned soon after with the robe, as well as a white tunic and a pair of white slippers.

"You really didn't have to get me all this," Arnold insisted.

"Darling, please. After dealing with those awful people, the very least you deserve is something to compensate for your traumatic experience. We don't want to give you the wrong impression of our city."

Arnold felt cornered. Then the man and woman fell silent, looking at him with faint smiles, as if they were waiting for Arnold to put his new clothes on immediately. He did.

"Here's an idea!" the woman exclaimed, as if just having a revelation. Arnold was beginning to realize how much she loved to talk. "Why don't you join us for dinner? You look like you haven't eaten in days."

"Fabulous idea, my love," the man said, taking an audible sip of his tea.

"Oh, I wouldn't want to impose," Arnold replied, when he really wanted to say, *I would like to run away.*

"Come," the woman said, ignoring Arnold's reservations and pushing him along. "We don't take no for an answer."

It struck him as odd that two strangers were so willing to take him in, but he reminded himself that for as much as the world is filled with bad people, it may be filled with just as many good. Perhaps this was what he needed to learn on his way to Kingdom.

He followed the couple through the white cobblestone streets of the city. All along the way, the man nodded and waved to people walking by, while the woman told Arnold stories of the city's lore. Every street and every shop had a story, and she somehow had a part in each one. She hardly finished one story before starting another.

The three of them arrived at the man and woman's home at the top of a steep hill, and walked through a gated area onto the front lawn. Their home was larger than any Arnold had seen below on the streets, and it was immediately apparent they were of a higher class.

Despite all the white things he'd seen in the city, it was their white lawn that really blew him away. He dropped down on one knee and brushed his hands over the blades of grass.

"How does it . . . Is it painted?" he asked.

"It just is," the man answered as he pulled out a long white pipe from his robe and then began to smoke. "The sun is yellow, the sky is blue, and our city is white."

"I've never seen anything like it before," Arnold said as he pinched a few blades of grass between his fingers.

"Careful," the man said, almost dropping his pipe from his lip. "The lawn requires a lot of upkeep, so if you could just . . . keep off it."

"Sorry," Arnold said as he got to his feet.

They continued past the lawn, making their way toward the front door. That was when Arnold saw it. Out in the backyard, behind a line of trees, was the unmistakable hue of black. He thought it was just his eyes playing tricks on him from the over-exposure to all the white. But it was there, a structure unlike anything else.

He wanted to ask them about it, but the man cut in.

"You can leave that in our garage," he said of the Tower.

They approached the house, and the woman walked inside while the man and Arnold walked to the garage. Arnold wheeled the Tower inside and parked it adjacent to a large wagon. It was a fancy white wagon, made of solid wood and with velvet drapes. Inside, the white upholstery was embroidered with a fancy pattern on the backseat. He thought his mother wouldn't like it. Too tacky.

"My mom would love this," Arnold said.

"She must have extraordinary taste," the man boasted.

"You lock this at night, right?" Arnold asked of the garage.

"Son, we lock the front gate," he said, and clapped him on the shoulder. "Nothing to worry about."

"Darling, would you show Arnold to his room?" the woman's voice echoed from within the house.

"Yes, dear."

"My room?"

"Yes, of course."

"That's very nice, but I shouldn't stay too long. I can find a nice place down in the city somewhere."

"Stop while you're ahead, son. It's getting late and you're already here. Stay the night and then you can leave refreshed in the morning. Besides, you'll want to wash up so your new clothes stay clean."

Arnold felt cornered again, thinking at this point it would be rude not to stay.

"Okay," he said, giving in.

Inside, the man led him up a spiral staircase to the second floor. The banister circled a large column and opened up into a hallway overlooking the main entrance. They walked to the end of the hall and arrived at the second-to-last door on the left. The man opened it to reveal a mostly empty room, save for a bed, a rug, and a dresser. The floor creaked as he stepped inside.

"The missus will come by and bring you some sheets," the man said. "Dinner will be ready shortly. I'm going to go have a smoke," he added, his pipe still resting on his lip.

"Okay."

Arnold closed the door behind him and turned on the light. It was blinding.

Too much white, he thought.

He was thankful he still had some color underneath his new white tunic; otherwise, he would go crazy. He took it off and lay down on the bare mattress. He hit it with a hard thud, expecting it to have some give, but it was incredibly firm, much firmer than he would've liked. But it was hard to complain; it was his first bed in weeks.

There was a ceiling fan circling above him and he stared into it. It spun at an intermittent speed while the neck gently swayed in circles. At any moment, he thought, it could pop loose and fall on him. At any moment.

He noticed something at the base of the fan, something that stood out among all the white. A small colored blotch. He stood up on the bed to get a better look.

There was a knock on the door.

He dropped to the edge of the bed and sat as the woman walked in holding a set of sheets.

"Settling in nicely, dear?"

"Yes, thank you for the room."

The woman went to closed the door behind her, leaving it open a sliver, and sat beside Arnold, placing the sheets on her other side.

"How do you like our home?"

"It's very nice. You have a very nice home. Very white."

He had never used the word *very* so many times before.

"Does it remind you of home?"

"Well, my house didn't really look like this. But there're some similarities, I guess."

The woman crossed her legs and folded her hands on her knee. "Interesting. Did you like your home?"

"I—I guess so?" Arnold replied.

The woman placed her hand on his shoulder and smiled at him, staring into his eyes. "Home isn't really home if you don't like where you are, right?"

"I guess not."

She got up from the bed and looked down at him. "Just something to think about."

Then she walked back to the door and opened it all the way. "Dinner will be ready soon. Why don't you go and wash up? There's a towel for you in the bathroom."

"Okay, sure. Thanks."

He sat there awkwardly until he realized the woman was waiting for him to get up and go to the bathroom before she left. He got up and slipped past her, his chest rubbing against her shoulder. Then she walked him to the bathroom.

"Don't be afraid to let me know if you need anything," she said.

"Okay."

Arnold closed the door behind him.

It was the first shower he'd had in a long time. He didn't realize it until he saw the gray water run past his feet and into the drain.

At least it's a different color, he thought.

After he washed himself, he kept the shower running and let the hot water rain down on him for a few more minutes. His hair clumped on his forehead and water trickled down his nose. He took in big gulps of water before turning the faucet off, then stood there, dripping. He put his hand up against the white-tiled wall and traced each finger with his other hand. He focused on the spaces between his fingers and wondered about all the spaces he'd put in between him and his old life and how the only space that mattered to him now was the one between him and Kingdom.

Arnold put on his new clothes again and rubbed his hair with the towel. The woman called from below, telling him that dinner was ready. For a second he could have sworn it was his own mother calling him.

On the table was a full spread, with a big roast chicken in the center and an array of side dishes from corner to corner. It was a long table, and the man and woman sat at opposite ends while Arnold sat in between them. Each dining set had three plates stacked on top of one another in increasing sizes, with special-sized utensils for every dish. The napkin was a high-quality cloth embroidered in elegant flowers. It looked like it had just been opened from a package, and Arnold felt bad for using it. They began passing around side dishes, and he noticed another table setting across from him.

Arnold spoke up. "Are we waiting for someone else?"

The man and woman caught each other's eyes.

"Oh yes," the woman seemed to pretend to remember. "Just a moment."

She excused herself from the table and walked out of the room and then out the back door.

"You'll have to excuse him," the man said, eating with his head down. "He's a bit of a strange one."

"Who is?"

"Our son." The man let out an exacerbating sigh.

"He's been outside this whole time?"

"He lives out there. His choice."

Arnold recalled the black structure behind the trees. The back door opened, and the woman walked in.

"Wipe your shoes before you walk inside."

Then she said it again. Her tone was much different the second time.

"Wipe them."

Arnold turned around in his chair as the man continued to eat by himself. In the doorway he could vaguely make out a silhouette in the dark night. The black figure stepped inside and closed the door behind him. It almost seemed to close on its own.

The woman sat back down at her seat while the black figure slowly walked around the table and sat across from Arnold.

The boy had on a dark cloak that draped past his feet. His hair was a black mop that hung over his eyes and shrouded his face. He was fair-skinned, but patches of bright white skin dotted his chin and knuckles in odd spotted patterns.

"Are you going to stare all night?" the cloaked figure asked.

"Sorry, I didn't mean to," Arnold replied.

The boy took a hard look at the table from end to end. He squished a finger down into a fluffy plate of mashed potatoes and rolled his eyes, shaking his head. Then he looked back and forth at the man and the woman before refocusing on Arnold.

"So, you're the new one?" he asked of Arnold.

"Cameron," the woman said, but as more of a reprimand than a declaration of his name. "Don't embarrass us in front of our guest."

"You'll have to excuse the boy," the man added. "He doesn't like company at the table."

Cameron started digging in. He stabbed the chicken breast with his fork and held the meat up to examine it before bringing the food back down to his plate and slicing it into cubes. The woman gave Cameron an irritated stare but smiled at Arnold.

"So tell me, Arnold . . . ," the woman began, composing herself. "How does a young man like yourself end up here?"

"Yes, and tell us about that thing you've been pushing around all day," the man added.

Arnold realized now that he was infinitely more comfortable talking to the Tower than about the Tower. The latter felt like telling a story that hadn't been fully written yet. It was messy, unorganized, and he wasn't all too confident in it. Learning how to talk about it was going to take time.

"Well, it's like a . . ."

Cameron picked his head up, suddenly curious.

"It's all the things I've ever owned," Arnold continued. "And I'm looking for a place to settle down in and sort of . . . start over. You know?"

The man and woman looked at each other, unsure of what to make of Arnold's story.

"Where are you going?" the woman asked.

"There's a place called Kingdom," Arnold continued as he gnawed on a piece of chicken. "Somewhere east. That's where I'm headed."

The woman seemed confused, expecting Arnold to say something else. "Right . . . but this thing you have with you . . . You said it has everything you own? As in, material possessions?" the woman asked while looking at Arnold, then at Cameron, then back at Arnold.

"Yes . . ."

"You must have been able to give away some of it to help others though, right?" the man chimed in.

Arnold looked around suspiciously. "Well, yeah, I guess so," Arnold said. "Sometimes."

Suddenly the woman's eyes lit up. "I knew you were special. I just knew it!" she exclaimed, practically jumping out of her seat to smack kisses on both of Arnold's cheeks.

The man shook his head with pride, as if he had just learned that his own son had finally become a man.

"Very admirable of you, son," the man added. "The mark of a good man is in his ability to be selfless when nobody is watching."

Arnold put on a forced smile.

"Well, aren't you just the nicest person around?" Cameron interjected.

Arnold had almost forgotten he was in the room.

"Cameron, don't ridicule him," the woman snapped.

"It's fine," Arnold insisted.

"Oh please, you don't have to entertain him," the woman said. "You're a good young man trying to make the world a better place."

"Well, sort of. It's a long story," Arnold said.

"And you've come a long way, correct?" the man asked.

Arnold could sense that the man and woman were trying to make sure Cameron didn't get any words in and that Arnold didn't go into too much detail. They wanted to keep up the perception that he had set out to "make the world a better place."

They continued to sing Arnold's praises while Cameron stomached his food in silence, giving Arnold calculated glances in the process. Cameron seemed to look right through him, numb to the barrage of words his parents threw at him. But Arnold knew it wasn't that easy. Words dug deeper than any blade or bullet. They burrowed under the skin and bruised the heart.

Given that he was eating their food and staying in their home, Arnold did his best to appease the man and woman, but he made it a point to finish his meal quickly and try to escape back to his room.

"Won't you stay and have dessert with us?" the woman asked, stopping Arnold as he tried to get out of his chair. Cornered again.

He stayed for dessert, which was apple cobbler, his favorite, and then excused himself from the table. Cameron had already dismissed himself long before dessert had even been mentioned, retreating to his cabin in the backyard.

When Arnold returned to his room, he kept the lights off and let the glow of the moon illuminate his face while he lay in bed. He thought about everything in front of him and wondered how much longer he had to go before reaching Kingdom. He thought about the lies he went along with during dinner and how easy it was. He worried if that was also true for Kingdom—that it, too, was some elaborate lie he was clinging to.

He got up and sat on the edge of the bed and let out a long sigh, listening to the breath escaping his mouth. It was that quiet.

He looked up at the ceiling fan, noticing that the dark spot that was still there. He stood up on the bed and put his face as close to it as he could. He scratched at it, and some white paint chipped away under his fingernail, revealing more darkness. It dawned on him that the whole room might have been painted white to cover up the dark color.

He walked toward the window to get a better look at the paint chip he'd picked from the ceiling. Looking out at the front yard, he caught a glimpse of an arm moving in the very corner of his view. He pressed his face up against the glass and saw the man standing on the front porch, leaning on the banister, pipe in his mouth. Arnold wondered if smoking was a hobby that calmed him down or if for him it was a status symbol. It seemed to Arnold that the man and the woman were very concerned with keeping up appearances. There was a toxic energy stewing in the house that reminded him of home, and Cameron seemed to be the product of that energy. He knew all too well how easy it was to become poisoned by association. Cameron's parents didn't understand the great power they held, just as Arnold's hadn't.

On their own, words hold an immense power, but no words hold more power than those of a parent.

He looked at his reflection in the window and repeated his plans to continue east in the morning. Nothing had changed, but he wanted to remind himself of that possible truth, of King-dom in the east.

He needed to prepare. Under shelter and rested, it was the perfect time to look for a few things he might need to keep handy, as well as continue to familiarize himself with the layout of the Tower. He also needed to clear his head.

He made his way downstairs, stopping just outside the kitchen. The man and woman were outside the front door, smoking quietly. Though their values seemed strange to him,

Arnold noticed that they got along more in their silence than his parents ever did with their words. He found himself feeling envious of how comfortable they were with each other.

He continued to the garage and opened the door. A rustling came from inside. Arnold flicked the light on and shielded his eyes as the bright white interior temporarily blinded him. He heard more rustling and caught a black figure dashing behind the Tower and some stacked boxes.

"Cameron?" Arnold called out.

There was a brief silence before Cameron emerged from the boxes.

"You caught me," he said sarcastically.

"What're you doing?"

"Wanted to see what *they* were so infatuated with. Wanted to see this thing for myself." Cameron eyed the Tower up and down. "Now I see it was just you they were smitten with. The idea of you. Just like all the rest."

Arnold stood there, intrigued by Cameron's eloquence. He could sense Cameron was smarter than he let on—smart, but suffering: a dangerous combination.

"This is quite a lot of stuff, though. You should be proud to come from such a wealthy family."

Arnold hesitated for a moment. "I wouldn't say wealthy. More like well-off."

"Do you like it?"

"Do I like what?"

"Coming from a well-off family."

"I've never thought of it before."

He thought about it all the time.

"I think about it sometimes," Cameron said. He paced around the room a bit and rested his head on the Tower. Arnold took notice of the white spots on his neck and ears that were revealed as his hair draped over the Tower. "I wonder what else we have in common."

There was a distinct shift in his tone now, but Arnold only took notice of it when Cameron's physical posture changed too. He was like a child who had forgotten why he was angry and suddenly wanted to be friends.

"I'm sure there are . . . other things," Arnold replied.

"So, you're going to Kingdom?"

It was harder for Arnold to lie to Cameron now that he looked like a sad puppy.

"Yeah. It's supposed to be . . . a great place."

"Kingdom . . ." He lifted his head off the Tower. "And you're taking this with you?"

"Yeah."

"Take *me* with you."

Arnold looked around, searching for an excuse. "Take you with me? I can't do that."

"But this thing," Cameron whined. "You could sneak me inside it."

"I'm sorry. I can't."

"It'll be easy. I can hide in here," Cameron said as he dug his hands into the Tower and pushed it apart, creating an opening.

"Stop! You're going to ruin it!" Arnold yelled at him.

"It'll be easy. Why won't you listen to me?"

Arnold grabbed Cameron by the arm and wrestled with him. "Cameron, stop!"

He pulled Cameron away from the Tower and Cameron pushed back, sending Arnold into the stack of boxes, kicking the cart as he fell. The Tower shifted as one of the wheels gave way and popped out of its caster. A few items flew out of the Tower and spilled onto the floor. Arnold jumped forward, using both hands to keep it upright.

"Stupid puppet! You and the rest of them!" Cameron yelled.

"Cameron!"

"I knew you were nothing special the moment I laid eyes on you. You're just another loser," he scolded Arnold.

Cameron stormed out of the garage, slamming the door behind him. Arnold was left alone with the damaged Tower.

He scanned the ground for the wheel that had popped loose. It was a few feet away from him. He stretched his foot out as far as he could and slid the wheel toward him, placing it flat on its side and back under the cart; it was enough to keep the Tower from tipping over.

Slowly, carefully, he backed away from it to see if it would stay up on its own. It did, and he let out a long sigh.

"If he ever lays a finger on you again . . ." Arnold whispered to the Tower.

He clenched his fist and looked down at his feet. His anger was nothing more than a blank scream in his head. Arnold didn't have that kind of violence in him. It would take something more real, more than he could possibly imagine, to ignite the coals of rage within him. Cameron was just a child, Arnold told himself, and he wasn't worth the energy.

He thought to ask the man for help in repairing the wheel but decided he'd rather be alone. Arnold kneeled down next to the empty caster, the toolbox open beside him, socket wrench, pliers, and screwdriver by his side. He tightened the bolts flanking the wheel and twirled the wrench in one hand, wiping beads of sweat from his brow with his other. Sometimes he was more adept at repairs than he gave himself credit for. He threw the tools into the toolbox and placed it back inside the Tower.

In the perch now, he grabbed a flashlight and began searching for supplies, the reason he'd gone there in the first place. It was a delicate procedure. He'd have to extract what he could without disrupting the integrity of the Tower. Twenty minutes later he'd been able to extract a toothbrush and toothpaste, a roll of toilet paper, a handful of loose bandages, two pairs of socks, and a half-eaten box of cheese crackers. He checked the expiration date.

With a stomach full of cheese crackers, he neatly stowed away the things he had been able to pull out. He was most excited about the toothbrush.

He walked up the steps and placed his hand on the doorknob, flicked the light switch off, and closed the door behind him, leaving the Tower in the dark.

As he approached his room, he saw that the door was open a crack. He stepped inside cautiously and saw the woman standing by the window, where Arnold had been standing earlier. It was as if she knew he had been watching her and the man before.

"I heard the commotion that Cameron caused downstairs," she said, still facing the window, her breath fogging up the glass in front of her. "I'm sorry you had to deal with him."

"It's okay."

She turned around and walked toward Arnold, placing her hand on his cheek. "You're a good boy, aren't you, Arnold?" she said as tears welled up in her eyes. "You must've been such a good boy."

Arnold could only stand there, stiff with the thought that any sudden word or movement might render her unstable. There was a stark contrast between the woman she was now and the woman at the dinner table. She was unveiled, vulnerable. She needed to be noticed.

"A good boy," she said again as she combed his hair to the side, away from his face.

Then she did what he thought she might do, a thought he'd had for a split second but then pushed to the back of his mind. She leaned in and kissed him, her dry, wrinkled lips sticking to his as she pulled away. It wasn't long, and in a blink he probably would have missed it. She looked straight down for a moment before removing herself from the room. Arnold continued to stand there in the dark, looking at the door. He pushed his hair to its original place, then walked back to the door and closed it slowly.

The road back home was truly as far away as it had ever been. He wondered if the closer he got to Kingdom, the more he would find himself caught in the affairs of others. He was beginning to realize that people were always going to see him, and by extension the Tower, the way they wanted to.

He couldn't just rely on himself to get to Kingdom anymore. He had to rely on the Tower, more than ever, despite any reservations he still had about it.

Kingdom was waiting for him, and the Tower, and the path there was only going to get more difficult. They had to work as a team to make it. Arnold now understood that he would have to be mindful of the people he met along the way. He had a responsibility to keep the Tower safe, and he would have to learn quickly which people were there to help him and which people would only want to take.

There was a moment, years ago. He thought about it as he lay there in the quiet dark, trying to fall asleep.

A giant blizzard had hit the day before, and the entire house was blanketed in over a foot of snow. It muted every sound. He was sitting on a couch adjacent to his father. They were waiting for a car to pick them up. It was dark out. Arnold wrestled to put on his boots, his movement hindered by the puffy jacket he wore. His father, doing the same, found the struggle of putting on boots in a big jacket just as difficult as his son. The friction in the room was palpable: of leather against cotton, nylon against nylon, and father against son.

They had been fighting for the past few days, his father demanding that his son grow up and start to take life more seriously. He went on about "the way of things" and how Arnold would never understand those things if he continued to act like such a child. The fighting lasted for days. But in that moment, there was a ceasefire in the war of words between them. A simple struggle that both could understand. A simple understanding of a simple task. And in it, they were able to share a smile, and a laugh.

Arnold took that moment and locked it away safely in his heart. It comforted him now as he lay there in the silence.

He'd wanted to say something to the woman after she'd kissed him. But the silence was easier. It spoke for him when all he wanted was to disappear.

He woke up early the next morning to prepare himself. He showered and put on fresh clothes he had grabbed from the Tower, as well as the white robe that the man and woman had bought him, figuring he'd wear it until he was outside the city.

There was a commotion downstairs, and he heard footsteps in the hallway. Arnold quickly jumped back into bed and closed his eyes, pretending to be asleep. Moments later the man opened the door, standing there for what seemed like an eternity. The door closed again and the man went back downstairs.

Arnold waited to hear the man's voice echoing from below before moving again. He dreaded having another conversation with him or the woman.

He got up and walked toward the window. The woman was outside, holding a tray and walking on the white lawn toward the side of the house. He waited until she disappeared from view before mustering up the will to leave the room. He slowly made his way downstairs to the kitchen and looked around, finding only plates with crumbs in the sink. The house was silent. He crept through the hallways, poking his head around corners. Finally he spoke.

"Hello?" he called out, waiting for an answer.

Nothing.

He walked out the front door, half expecting the woman to be back, sharing a smoke with the man, but again they were nowhere to be found.

An overwhelming sense of relief washed over him. He made his way to the garage, where sunlight filled the room and blanketed the Tower. He pushed a button on the wall near the door, and the garage door lifted up. He grabbed the Tower and wheeled it out onto the driveway and made his way to the front gate.

Then he saw it again: that black dot in the sea of white, the unmistakable darkness. He thought about Cameron. Arnold had something for him, something he'd thought of that morning, and he couldn't leave until he gave it to him.

He wheeled the Tower up to Cameron's shack and parked it just outside the door. The shack had been crudely put together with old wood and rusted nails. It was quiet outside, with just the rustling of trees around him. He approached the front door to find it was already half open, and looked around to see if Cameron was somewhere close by, but he saw no one. It wouldn't have been hard to spot him. Arnold slowly opened the door the rest of the way and walked in.

It was significantly darker inside than anywhere in the man and woman's home, darker than anywhere else in the entire city, for that matter. There were piles of junk all over the floor: broken figurines, small pieces of wooden furniture, bent pieces of metal, and twisted heaps of string and wire. He weaved through the cluttered mess of the shack. The floor creaked with every step, and the walls were cracked, the veneer peeling all over. This wasn't a luxurious cabin renovated for Cameron to live in; this was a shed in the woods with a bed in it.

"What're *you* doing here?" a voice called out from the shadows, startling Arnold.

Cameron was sitting in a chair in the far corner, facing the front door. He'd seen Arnold's every move, and in that moment, Arnold was glad he hadn't said or done anything to compromise himself.

"Sorry, your door was open. I didn't know you were here."

"Well, I'm right here. And now you are too. What do you want?" Cameron was noticeably out of breath.

"I came here to give you this," Arnold said as he reached into his robe.

He pulled out a red sweater with white stripes, folded neatly in a square, and extended it to him. Cameron got up from his chair and slowly walked toward Arnold. Every step creaked.

He grabbed the sweater from Arnold's hand and looked at it, uncertain of what to make of it.

"Open it," Arnold said.

Cameron flipped the sweater over and undid the sleeves, revealing a notebook with a pen poking out of the top.

"I know it can be hard at times . . . ," Arnold began. "But a notebook is a great way to get your thoughts out. It listens when nobody else will. And I think you'll like that sweater, too. It belonged to my dad."

A smile crept up at the corners of Arnold's mouth. Cameron turned around and walked back toward his chair. He stood there for a moment, and there was an awkward silence. Cameron opened the notebook and thumbed through the empty blue-lined pages.

"What do you know?" Cameron finally asked.

"Huh?"

"What do you know about nobody listening to you?"

Arnold swallowed a lump in his throat. "More than you might think, Cameron."

Cameron turned around again and took a few steps toward Arnold before winding his arm back and hurling the sweater and notebook at Arnold's head. Arnold ducked out of the way, and the items landed on a pile of Cameron's stuff with a loud crash as it toppled over.

"Get out of here!" Cameron yelled at him. "I'm not some pushover you can dump your garbage on."

"Cameron . . ." Arnold said, trying to stay composed but reeling a bit now.

"You think you can just show up to my house and start shoving this crap in my face?" he continued. "You don't know anything. You think you do, but you don't."

"I'm just trying to help you," Arnold replied, shaking.

"I didn't ask for your help," Cameron barked back, pointing a finger in Arnold's face. "I don't need your help. I don't need anyone's help. You're the one who needs help."

"I'm sorry, Cameron. You don't have to—"

"Look around you. This darkness here, this is what's real. I'm the realest one here. I'm not blinded by all the light. I look into the darkness and see the truth."

Arnold remained still. He wasn't exactly sure what Cameron was talking about, but he sensed that what he was saying had been brewing in him for a long time.

"You, and that *thing* of yours have no place here, so just get out."

The fiery passion in Cameron's eyes paralyzed Arnold.

"Get out!"

Cameron had no sooner exhaled his last word than the air in between the two boys expanded and a rush of heat barraged Arnold's face. An immense pressure pushed against him, catapulting him backward onto another pile of Cameron's stuff. Arnold lay there for a moment, petrified.

Cameron had retracted his finger and now slowly looked down at his hand, then at his palms, in awe. Arnold waited for Cameron to say something, but he didn't.

"What the hell was that?" Arnold exclaimed.

Cameron remained silent, stepping backward until he, too, sat down on a pile of junk. He continued to stare at his palms. Then, finally, he looked up at Arnold, his mouth agape.

Before another word was spoken, Arnold quickly got to his feet, picking up the things Cameron had thrown at him, and ran out of the shack. He kicked the brake of the Tower, throwing his things up into the perch, and swiftly pushed the Tower down to the bottom of the hill until he was back in the city again. He walked as fast as he could through the streets while people gave him looks and yelled at him in the language he didn't understand, probably telling him to slow down. But he paid no attention to them. There was nothing anyone could say to him in that moment to make him feel more frightened than he already was.

He neared the edge of the city entrance and moved over to the side of the road to catch his breath.

What was that? he thought. *It was like he . . . pushed me back with an invisible object or something. How can that be?*

Arnold didn't know what to make of it. In some bizarre fusion of Cameron's anger and Arnold's inability to understand him, Cameron had pushed him with some sort of kinetic force. It was as if he had unlocked it right before Arnold's eyes. Had it been a coincidence? Divine intervention? There was no way of knowing, but Arnold wasn't going to stay around long enough to find out.

He looked out beyond the city's border, realizing he'd have to trek through the torrential rains once again in order to leave. He reached up into the perch and pulled out the tarp, his hands shaking. As he began to cover the Tower with the tarp, he saw a small boy playing on the street, drawing in the ground with a wooden stick. Arnold admired the simplicity of the act, longing to switch places with the boy. Instead he climbed up into the perch again and pulled out the sweater meant for Cameron. He walked up to the boy on the street and kneeled down in front of him. The boy raised his head, pure innocence on his face.

"Hey," Arnold said as he handed the sweater to him. "You like this?"

The child nodded.

"Good. You can have it."

The boy looked at the sweater in confusion. It may have been the first time he'd ever seen the color red in his life.

With that, Arnold pushed the Tower forward, past the outer walls of the city. The boy stood up and watched him leave, throwing the sweater over his head and pulling it down to his waist. It hung to his knees, the sleeves draping past his fingers.

Arnold wheeled the Tower forward and propped the excess tarp above his head. He was prepared for the storm, knowing in his heart that the harder he pushed, the easier it would be to make his way out of it. He had to push forward, for Kingdom. As long as he and the Tower were together, he knew he could make it there.

The silhouette of the Tower grew smaller in the black eyes behind the windowpane. A fist clenched and a hot breath fogged up the glass. Soon, all intentions would be realized.

5

THE STRANGER

"Let me out!" Cameron yelled, pounding on a wooden door with his fists. The door shook on its rusty hinges.

There was no answer.

He yelled again, then quickly pulled his hand to his face, where his cheeks seethed in pain from fresh cuts. Cameron ran a finger along his cheek. They were wet with spots of blood.

He banged on the door again, but still there was no answer.

In the backyard of the home where the man and woman lived, against the white brick wall that lined the rear of the house, two white doors led to a cellar. The doors were closed, sealed by a padlock. Inside this dark cellar was another door, locked with a key, that led to an even smaller room. In this room, was Cameron.

His breathing grew heavy, claustrophobia setting in.

"Don't be afraid," a voice whispered in the darkness.

Cameron quickly turned around, pressing his back up against the door. "W-who's there?" he called out, shaking.

"Don't be afraid," the voice repeated. "I won't harm you."

"Who are you?"

"A friend."

"I don't have friends."

"Me neither."

Cameron swallowed a lump in his throat.

"Will you be my friend?" the voice asked, unprovoked.

"I can't even see you."

"Yes, you can. Open your eyes."

Cameron opened his eyes wider, trying to see anything in the room. "They're open," he said.

"Do you see me now?"

"No."

"That's okay," the voice assured. "I can see you."

A shiver ran down Cameron's spine. "What do you want?"

"What do *you* want?" the voice repeated.

"I want to get out of here."

"Me too," the voice said.

"Why do you want to get out of here?"

The room went silent.

"Hello?" Cameron asked.

"To make them suffer," the voice whispered, noticeably rougher.

"Make who suffer?"

It was quiet again. Cameron slowly stepped forward into the room and felt around for the person who was speaking to him. He made his way to the back wall and sat down. He felt a draft suddenly, but his ears began to warm up.

"Everyone," the voice whispered into his ear. Cameron felt the voice pressing up against him. "How does that sound?"

"Everyone?"

"The ones who deserve it," the voice said.

"And who are they?"

"Everyone," the voice whispered again.

A smile crept onto Cameron's face.

It was the first of many nights he'd spent in the quiet dark of the cellar, mending his wounds, expanding the black hole in his mind with shadowy thoughts. Here he learned to become more in tune with these thoughts, and came to understand that he had an easier time in the darkness than he did in a city that was nothing but white. He convinced himself that the real terrors in life happened in the light, and it was only in darkness where he could truly be himself.

The man and woman could never understand this and, by extension, could never understand Cameron himself. That's why they preferred to keep him, their greatest misfortune, locked up, sometimes for days at a time. They punished him, not knowing that in the process, they were creating something they would one day have no power over.

In the solitary of his shack was where Cameron preferred to spend most of his time. He stayed away from his parents as much as he could, focusing instead on his hobbies. He would spend all day reading, writing, carving wooden figures of characters from his favorite books, roaming the white forest that surrounded his shack, and climbing the surrounding hills on the outskirts of the city, watching people go about their days. He never truly felt like a member of the city, and so he preferred the solitude. When he did make visits to the city, he would wait until the crowds dissipated, or he would go early before anyone was awake.

When the sun set and the sky turned dark, it meant dinnertime. Every evening the dining room filled with a muted haze, where the man read his paper and puffed on his pipe and the woman prattled on about something inconsequential that had happened in the city that day. The woman brought home the same meal every night from a small shop in the poor district of the city. And while the man and woman had grown accustomed to the taste, their tongues having turned gray many years ago, Cameron had not. Every night he begrudgingly swallowed gray chunks of meat that dissolved like chalk in his mouth.

It was only when his mother and father invited a new stranger to spend the night that Cameron was able to enjoy a decent meal. Even though it was never meant for him.

Those nights always played out in the same way. The stranger would come at the behest of the man and the woman, dressed in a brand-new outfit that they had just purchased for him. He would spend the night, sometimes more than one, and slowly, the man and woman would turn him into their child, the one they really wanted. Cameron was used to this charade, and after years of experiencing it firsthand, he preferred to stay out of it. He didn't want to participate in the delusions of his parents anymore.

But it wasn't always that easy, and sometimes he found it hard to ignore their behavior. On those nights, just after the stranger had left, dinner always ended with confrontation.

"I can't eat this. I don't want to eat this food," Cameron would say.

"Cameron, groceries can get very expensive. Don't you care about this family?" the woman would ask in a monotone voice.

"You're right. I guess I'll have to wait for another stranger to end up on our doorstep for you to find the money to pay for groceries."

Then he would throw his utensils at the table and knock over his glass. The man would continue to smoke and read his paper.

Cameron would continue his childish fit, throwing his chair to the ground or kicking the man's chair until he got mad.

When this happened, the man would neatly fold his newspaper, place it on the table, get up from his chair, and grab Cameron by his shirt collar. With great force, he'd throw him down to the ground, dragging him by his shirt out the front door, through dirt and grass and around to the cellar doors in the backyard. He would lift the boy to his feet. Cameron would continue to squirm and throw a tantrum. Then would come a slap. Then another.

Another.

Another.

Harder.

Again.

Again.

Blistered cheeks created deep valleys of red water.

Afterward, the man would fling the cellar doors open, throw Cameron over his shoulder, and open another door at the bottom of the stairs. There, the man would throw Cameron down and lock the door behind him before returning to his dinner as if nothing had happened.

This routine continued for years.

Until the day Cameron met Arnold.

After their altercation in Cameron's shack, Cameron showed up to the night's dinner with a renewed spirit. He was at the table before anyone else, a first for him.

"Oh, Cameron . . . you're . . . early to dinner," the woman said, caught off guard by his presence.

"I worked up an appetite today," Cameron replied, grinning.

"Yes, you did," the woman said as she set the table. "You gave that boy quite a scare last night. So much so that he ran away without saying goodbye."

Cameron said nothing, staring out across the table, lost in thought. The woman finished setting the table and laying out the food, and the man came into the kitchen, assuming his usual position in front of his paper. They started eating, and where the woman would normally have started talking about her day, tonight she was unusually quiet.

After a few minutes of silence she said, pouting, "I do wish that boy would have stayed or said goodbye."

"Yes, a shame," the man said, his voice muffled behind the newspaper.

"He was such a determined boy too. Such desire in his heart."

"Yes, a good head on that one," the man replied.

The woman sighed, looking down at her plate, almost to the point of tears. Cameron, in between them, gnawed at his chicken, eating quickly.

"Do you think he will miss us?" the woman asked, looking up.

"Yes, I'm sure," the man replied.

"He was so handsome, too," the woman went on.

"Mm, yes."

"And kind . . ."

"Mm . . ."

The woman looked down at her plate again, searching for the will to talk about something else.

"How mad," Cameron finally spoke up.

The woman lifted her head, her eyes wide, while the man slowly lowered his paper, pipe hanging on the edge of his lip.

"What did you say?" the woman asked.

Cameron remained silent.

"Answer your mother," the man said sternly.

"I said, *how mad* can you both be?" Cameron repeated. "To admire a person like him."

"What?" the woman scoffed. "That young man was a gentle, kind soul with a noble purpose in his life."

"And yet you don't question how he came to possess all of his family's things," Cameron said. "How do you think that happened?"

His father scoffed and shook his head. "You just amaze me with your continued ignorance," he snarled. "If you were half the man he was, you would see the decency in his effort to make the people around him happy. He doesn't sit in a dark room and waste his life away. He's out there; he's doing something. He actually cares."

"How can you even say something like that, Cameron?" the woman asked. "Instead of criticizing him, why don't you use him as an example for yourself?"

Cameron went silent again. He thought about all the things he wanted to say, but knew he had more important matters to attend to. At the moment, his only concern was to get through to the end of dinner so he could exercise his new ability.

Hours later, Cameron left his shack to sneak back into the house. It was late, and his parents had already gone to bed. He entered through the kitchen and made his way upstairs, to the man and woman's bedroom. He crept up the staircase and turned left, down the opposite end of the hall where Arnold had stayed. It was quiet. The man and woman's door was left open a sliver and Cameron peeked in. They slept in the same bed and lay close to each other. He gently pushed the door open, just enough to slip in undetected.

His objective was the bedside table next to the man. Inside was a key that would grant him access to the cellar in the backyard. He approached the bed and stood over the two of them, watching them breathe. He could have stood there all night, studying every inch of their vulnerable bodies, but tonight was different.

Instead he reached for the drawer and gently pulled at the handle. He placed his hand inside and felt around for the ring of keys that opened the cellar doors. To his surprise, they were right on top of a stack of papers, and he accidentally brushed against them. They made a loud clinking noise and he clenched his eyes shut, freezing in place.

The man turned over on his side, facing Cameron now. Cameron opened his eyes again, slowly, and looked back at the man. His eyes were still closed. Cameron let out a nervous breath and quickly grabbed the keys, closing the drawer quietly.

He backed out of the room and stared into the darkness, wondering if something would alert the man and woman of his presence and wake them up. But nothing happened, and Cameron slowly closed the door to its original position, giving the man and woman one final look through the crack in the door.

In the cellar again, Cameron stood in the center of the room and looked around. This time felt different. He felt different. He wanted to be here.

"I have something to show you," Cameron called out in the darkness.

There was no response.

"Hello?"

Still nothing.

Cameron paced around the room, rubbing his hand against the concrete walls.

"You'll want to see this," he continued. "I promise."

Still there was no answer. Cameron walked back into the middle of the room. In the darkness, he stared in the direction of the entrance. Slowly, he lifted his hand up and concentrated on the lock on the other side of the door. He focused, trying his best to imagine the lock turning and releasing so he could escape. His arm shook and he strained his face. Nothing happened, and finally he released his force and exhaled. He looked at his hands.

"Why isn't it working?" he asked himself. He tried again and still, nothing happened.

He crawled into the corner of the room and sat with his head down, thinking. He ran through his confrontation with Arnold, the nature of their exchange and what he had felt when he had pushed Arnold.

"I'm waiting," a voice materialized in the cellar.

Cameron picked his head up. "You're here."

"Yes. I'm always here."

"Why didn't you say anything before?"

The cellar went quiet again and Cameron stood up. "Hey! You can't just ignore me whenever you want. I'm stronger now."

"Show me," the voice demanded.

Cameron lifted his hand up again and concentrated on the door once more. He tensed his arm until it shook, but nothing happened.

"I— It's not working," Cameron said, visibly frustrated.

"Liar," the voice growled at him.

"I'm not lying!" Cameron yelled.

"Where does your strength come from?"

"I don't know," Cameron answered, frustrated.

"Who suffers now?"

Cameron placed his hand over his mouth, thinking again.

"Arnold?" he finally said.

"Arnold . . ." the voice answered.

"It was him. I made him suffer."

"Yes . . ."

"But he's nobody. That thief can't be the reason. There have been many like him before."

"What makes him different?" the voice asked.

Cameron sat down and crossed his legs, dipping his head low, letting his hair cascade over his face.

"Nothing. He isn't special."

The voice went silent again as Cameron continued to think.

"Maybe it was that *thing* . . . ?"

"Yes . . ." the voice returned.

"It's the outlier."

"You made *it* suffer."

"I did. . . ."

"And then you felt it. Your true potential. What they don't want you to have."

"Yes . . ."

"You know what to do."

"Make it suffer."

"Yes."

"What if he gets in the way?"

"Make *them* suffer."

Cameron sat still for a while before standing up and heading for the door. He placed the key into the lock and turned it, then stopped.

"But I don't know where he is. How will I find him?"

A chill swept through the room and ran down his spine. Cameron turned around. In the corner, at the back of the room, a dark haze took shape, growing tall, like a person. Cameron's heart began to beat faster, his breaths becoming sporadic. He quickly turned around and opened the door, closing it behind him. He shook his head, telling himself he was seeing things.

Though he had found his way out of the cellar himself, it was not in the way he had hoped. He still had work to do and so he returned to his shack.

Here, he glazed over a multitude of piles on the ground. He walked to the back storage closet near the end of the shack. It was a cluttered mess of machines, pipes, and cobwebs, and a single lightbulb overhead with a string attached. In the pile of machines, a handle of a wheelbarrow stuck out. He lifted his hand once more, focusing on it, trying to pry the wheelbarrow loose with his mind, but nothing happened. Instead Cameron reached into the pile to grab it. He pulled hard as tangled blades and wires held it down. He kicked some of the garbage away, reaching farther into the pile to grab the wheelbarrow from the other side. As he reached in, he caught the side of a lawn mower blade and sliced his hand. He immediately pulled it back and started sucking on the wound, stomping on the pile in a rage as his hand bled. Finally the item came loose, and the rest of the machinery in the closet toppled over.

Cameron rolled the newly relinquished wheelbarrow to his den, where the piles of junk lay. Before he could make the journey to find Arnold, he had to prepare. And despite his goal to destroy it, the Tower had given him the idea to create something he could store supplies in for his own journey.

He began the process of assembly. He quickly piled his things on top of one another, as each added layer spilled over the sides. There was no form or tactic to it; he grabbed handful after handful and threw each item into the wheelbarrow, all the while waiting for his tower to take shape. He grew more frustrated as every handful fell to the ground, but he kept trying, defiant.

No matter how much he piled up or how carefully he tried to assemble it, his tower never formed. As the futility of his task became evident, his frustration clouded his mind, quickly turning to self-pity, and then to anger. He kicked the wheelbarrow over. In a rage, he began picking up piles of junk and throwing them across the room. He then grabbed the wheelbarrow by the handles and, with all his might, threw it across the room. It landed next to the front door with a crash.

He retreated to a corner of the room, his head between his knees, short of breath. Light shone in from a window, creating a spotlight on his fake tower as he sat in darkness. It was a crumbling mess. If he was going to create his own tower, he needed more than what he had in his shack. He had to go back into town. He had to acquire the tools necessary to build it.

He stumbled to his feet and made for the front door. Dawn was just beginning to break, and by the time he made it to the city, it was daytime.

Shops began opening and people started leaving their homes, many of them heading to work. Cameron roamed the streets, looking for a shop that could sell him a larger wheelbarrow. That was where he would start.

He found his way to one of the gates leading out of the city and into the canyon below. As he turned a corner, he spotted a small boy playing in the dirt.

He was wearing a bright red sweater with white stripes.

"Hey, you!" he called to the boy. "Where did you get that sweater?"

The boy pointed to the gates, toward the road to the canyon.

Cameron turned to face the road. The direction was east, toward a path that led down the mountain and into the storm wall that protected the city. He looked closer, focusing on the wall of rain. Scattered bolts of lightning hurtled across the sky like fissures from an earthquake.

"Arnold . . . Kingdom . . ."

There was no easing into it. He would have to take the storm head-on.

And even though the Tower was far out of sight, he now knew where to go to find it. One way or another, Cameron would get his power back. He looked down at his hands again, dried blood smeared on one of his palms, and then out toward the storm once more.

I'll find you, he thought. *And I'll take back what's mine.*

6

PERCEPTIONS

The Blue house was a different place on the weekends than it was on weekdays. On Friday and Saturday nights Mr. and Mrs. Blue went out on the town. A new show, their favorite restaurant, a friend's birthday: these were the rare times when they did things together. Arnold remembered the uneasiness in the air inside the house on those nights and how everything was an orchestra of chaos. Mr. Blue was always the first to get dressed. He would don one of his single-button linen jackets and a pair of genuine leather oxfords but would quickly change into something completely different after Mrs. Blue had shared her disdain for his outfit.

Mrs. Blue was all for flair. It wasn't about who they were going to see; it was about what those people were going to see.

Her outfit dictated the night, and if it wasn't the right outfit, it wasn't going to be a good night. Mr. Blue usually stayed out of her way, opting to wait downstairs while she figured things out.

All the while Mrs. Blue tore her closet apart, Arnold hid in the shadows, watching her from the doorway. In her vortex of disarray, she'd fail to hear him or even feel his presence. He'd look on as she carefully placed her foot in each shoe and rotated her feet in the mirror's reflection. She'd lift a foot up to her knee in an attempt to fasten the straps, but aging muscles created a force field that quickly pushed her back. She'd groan and begin the process of judging all the things she wished she could change about herself, and Arnold wished he could tell her she didn't need to change a thing. But she would rattle on, from the hair she could never keep straight to the weight she could never keep off to the lines on her face that only dug deeper.

He understood her want to feel good about herself and what she wore, but it was more than that. It was *too* important to her. On those nights, when she had to present herself to the outside world, she became a black hole, sucking in all the life around her. She was consumed with scrutinizing herself, and instead took it out on the things she didn't have and the people she took for granted.

Arnold kept tabs of her mental checklist, all the while wishing he were brave enough to tell her that everything was okay, that she was okay, that she was fine the way she was and with what she had. He wanted to steal a hug and tell her everything he had built up in his head for years.

But the opportunity always passed. She'd call out to Mr. Blue and tell him that they'd have to postpone the evening because nothing fit or she had nothing new to wear. Then Arnold would slip away before she would notice, tiptoeing back to his room. There, he would wish for any kind of enlightenment to strike her, or a moment of bravery to strike him. But it never did.

Arnold held up the vanity mirror to get a good look at himself. There was an unfamiliar face staring back at him, with features old and new. His skin was darker, the color akin to the tans he got on the weekend beach trips from his childhood, and dozens of freckles dotted his nose and cheeks. They mapped a path to forgotten years of youthful happiness.

His blond hair had grown long and was tangled with grease. He constantly had to push it to the side and out of his eyes. It was an unfamiliar motion to him; his whole life he had kept his hair short, the way his mother liked it. The color, which had been bleached by the sun, was unfamiliar as well.

The sun reflected from the mirror into his eyes, and he recalled all the weekends he'd spent indoors back home.

A square block of light would penetrate through the window and ink the floor as he watched daytime television. He would stick his foot out to catch the sun while he sat on the couch. Sometimes he would move to the floor and let the warmth seep into his skin and touch his bones. When the sunlight reached the front step of his porch, he would sit there, too, watching people go by as they walked dogs, jogged, rode bikes. Then he'd go inside until dusk came, and the sadness of the setting sun was all he could think about.

Arnold looked away from the mirror and stowed it inside the Tower. On the plank now, he leaned back against the cart and looked up as the Tower swayed gently in the breeze. For the past two nights, he'd been camping out near a lake at the edge of a mountain range. He had started his journey up the mountain, thinking it would be an easy trip, but it turned out to be way more tumultuous than he'd expected.

He decided to detour around the mountain instead, through a dense forest. It rained that whole day, a steady, harassing rain, and Arnold was forced to stop every few minutes to clean away foliage that had gotten lodged in the metal plates of the Tower's wheels. He realized the cart was not meant to fight through the elements on a daily basis. It was just a shopping cart. He thought it was a miracle it had even lasted this long.

The lake was a welcome relief. At the other end of it, the forest continued, so he decided to make camp near the shore until he was ready to do it all again. But two days had passed, and he felt no more ready to head back into the forest.

He planned a third night at the lake and thought to use the extra time to find some food, to avoid eating through his supply. But Arnold was no hunter, not even close. He thought about going out to the edge of the lake to cast a line, remembering the fishing trips he used to take with his father to a lake up north. Then he thought about bait. Then he decided not to. The idea of jabbing a living creature with a sharp hook, even something as small as a worm, had never sat well with him. During those trips he had squirmed with guilt as a shriveling worm on the end of his line did the same, and it filled him with remorse. It was always his dad's job to restock the hook, and after so many times when Arnold had refused to man up, the trips eventually came to a halt. He had forgotten how to fish.

He decided instead to head back into the forest and look for berries or nuts he could forage. After about an hour of searching, he hadn't found anything. The forest was still damp from the full day of rain, making it hard to trudge through. He decided then that once the ground had dried enough, he'd keep heading east.

Two more days passed.

On the fifth night, Arnold stepped into the tree line to test the soil. It was dark, but he had a fire going at his campsite near the Tower. The soft glow of the flames exposed the contour of its shape. He walked in circles, listening to the crunch of leaves on the ground. Tomorrow he'd try again.

He stepped out of the forest and walked back toward the lake. He was surrounded by the sounds of crickets chirping, distant animals cooing, and frogs croaking by the water. They were sounds that could lull a man to sleep.

He was halfway back to the Tower when he heard the familiar sound of crunching leaves again. He stopped to look down at his feet. He stared at the flat rock underneath him, then quickly turned around to face the tree line. The crunching sound was coming toward him.

Something was out there.

He backed away slowly as the terror of having to defend himself against a wild animal sent his heart racing. He took another step into a small depression and lost his balance, falling onto his back. He quickly rolled onto his stomach and locked his eyes on the tree line. Whatever it was, he was going to hide from it.

He heard voices now. A man. Two men. They were getting closer. Whispers between the two that he couldn't make out.

Finally they broke through the trees and Arnold saw them: two men, one with a beard, both carrying loaded rucksacks. One man was using a long walking stick. They stood at the edge of the forest.

"You see that?" the man with the stick called out. He pointed to Arnold's fire.

"Maybe somebody's here already," the bearded man responded as he stopped to clean off his boots with his hands. They began walking toward Arnold's camp.

The fire, Arnold thought. *Stupid.*

As he was about to stand up, he heard another voice echoing from inside the forest. It was a woman's voice. It called out to the two men.

"You guys, I told you you're moving too fast! I almost lost you in there."

The two men stopped to wait for the woman. The man with the stick lifted it above his head with two hands and stretched his torso from side to side. Arnold looked on, working up the courage to come out of hiding. He thought about how foolish he'd feel if they saw him lying there on his stomach, and found his moment of bravery.

"Hello there," Arnold called out as he stood up. The two men turned to face him.

"H-hey, who's there?" the man with the walking stick said. "We don't mean any harm."

"Are you lost?" Arnold asked.

"Sort of. We've been out in the forest all day."

"Where are you going?"

"Southeast."

"Well, you're sort of in the right place."

Arnold introduced himself to the three strangers. They were backpackers, he learned, heading to a town said to be completely engulfed by peach trees.

"Peach trees?" Arnold asked, puzzled at the thought of it.

"Trees that have been growing there for over a thousand years," the woman said. "Or something like that."

"And a mass grave surrounds those trees," the man with the walking stick added.

"A mass grave?"

"A lot of people fought and died to take that town back in the day," the man with the walking stick continued. "Wars fought for resources."

"Yeah, wars fought for peaches," the woman said.

Arnold thought about it for a moment. "Wars have been fought over lesser things, I guess." He surprised himself with his own wisdom.

The four spent the night by the lake, where Arnold introduced them to the Tower. He explained to them about his journey to head east toward Kingdom and they agreed to travel together as far as the other end of the forest.

The sun rose and Arnold was the last to get up. The others had the fire going again and breakfast cooking.

"Smells good," Arnold said.

"Fried veggie sausage and dehydrated soy milk to wash it down," the man with the walking stick said. He looked over at the woman.

"I'm a vegetarian," the woman said as she sat on a log, forcefully shoving clothes back into her rucksack.

"Well, it smells good enough."

The woman struggled to find more space in her bag.

"You know, if you folded your clothes, you'd have a lot more room," Arnold suggested.

She let out a loud *ugh*. "I know. I always get like this when I'm traveling."

"If you had a boyfriend, he would probably be horrified," the bearded man boasted.

"Yeah, my last boyfriend was pretty turned off by it."

The bearded man shrugged as if to say, *I told you so.*

"But he's not my boyfriend anymore," she said defiantly as she made no attempt to fold her clothes.

The bearded man kept quiet. The sizzle of the veggie sausage helped fill the awkward silence while the man with the walking stick gave Arnold a look as if to say, *Stay out of it.*

The four of them ate and washed the meal down with the rehydrated soy milk. Before they left, Arnold asked if he could be second to last in their march so two of them could carve a path for the Tower while the third hung back in case it got stuck. They agreed, and Arnold began to wonder what he could give to the travelers once they parted ways.

The ground was dry now and Arnold had a caravan. The second trudge through the forest proved to be much easier, and Arnold felt embarrassed for waiting so long to venture out. His group assured him that it was okay and that they were glad to have run into him.

They were interested in the Tower and asked him a lot of questions about it. It was the first time he'd had to talk about it for more than a couple of minutes. He realized things he'd never thought of just by speaking about the Tower more. He learned how important it was to him. He learned how little he actually knew of all its parts, and he learned that although the things it was made of were what made him angry, the Tower itself did not. The idea was something he didn't fully understand yet.

Hours passed as the group continued through the forest. Arnold and the woman had been talking for most of the way. She told him her name was Charlotte and he told her he liked her name. Meanwhile, the two men charged ahead, talking about their favorite beers and the video games they missed from back home. Home for them was somewhere out west, not far from where Arnold came from. He wondered who had been traveling the longest.

The man with the walking stick appeared suddenly, waving at them. "Guys, you gotta come see this."

"What is it?" Charlotte called back.

"Just hurry up!"

Arnold and Charlotte rushed over as fast as the Tower allowed them. The men climbed up a big boulder and went down the other side. When they got there, there was no clear way to get the Tower over.

Charlotte looked at the boulder, then back at Arnold, frowning.

"It's fine," Arnold ensured her. "Go see what they found."

"Hang on," she said, and then pulled herself up the boulder and down the other side.

Arnold heard her call out to the men as he stood impatiently next to the Tower. He looked for some way to bring it around.

Finally a voice came from above.

"The ol' ball and chain, huh?"

It was the man with the walking stick, standing on top of the boulder. He hopped down next to Arnold. Charlotte and the bearded man followed.

"Let's get this thing of yours up there."

Together, the four of them picked the Tower up just long enough to get it over the boulder. The two men pulled it while Arnold and Charlotte pushed it up the side. Under different circumstances, he wouldn't have allowed anyone else to move the Tower, but he trusted them.

Over the rocks, he saw what all the commotion was about. There was a waterfall splashing into a pool of white foamy water, making a magnificent roar. The men were elated, having immediately removed everything but their underwear. They dove into the pool with loud yelps and shouts of liberation.

Charlotte threw down her pack and began pulling off her boots as Arnold nervously looked away and checked the cart for any damage. He pretended to occupy himself with the Tower by picking at some rust on the grates, but she paid him no mind as she unbuttoned her jeans and slid them down to her ankles, lifting each leg out. She glistened with sweat, and Arnold's heart raced. He noticed the numerous birthmarks dotting her legs, her thighs, her butt. She crossed her arms and lifted her tank top from the bottom, up over her head. It passed over her long black hair and she dropped the shirt to her feet. Between her shoulder blades nested a dandelion tattoo whose dozens of white feathery seeds had been uprooted by a gust of wind. They reached across her skin, momentarily stealing his attention away from the rest of her body. She turned around and caught him staring at her pear-shaped figure.

"Coming?" she asked coyly.

Her eyes pierced him, and a rush of blood filled his chest.

"Yeah, I'll meet you guys in a second," he said, his voice cracking.

He had no intention of actually joining them.

Arnold was not the type to go out to a lake and jump in wearing nothing but his underwear, nor was he the type to sit in a circle around a campfire and tell stories or wander through a forest with strangers. Skinny-dipping for him was walking around his house without a shirt on, wandering through a forest was cutting through a park on his way home from school, and sitting around a fire with strangers was staring at the stovetop as he cooked eggs in the morning, a glaze over his eyes.

Charlotte reached behind her back and unhooked her bra, gently tossing it to the side. She shivered, and goose bumps rose up her spine and neck and inched onto her shoulders.

Suddenly Arnold had every intention of joining them.

He feverishly unbuckled his belt and dropped his pants, lifting his shirt over his head and throwing it to the ground. Charlotte was in the water already, the surface clinging to the handles of her hips. She dove in. Arnold followed behind and dipped his feet in the water. It was icy, so he eased himself in gently. Charlotte emerged from below and rubbed the water from her eyes. Her long black hair stuck to her back in a perfectly straight line. She turned around and faced him. Arnold stopped himself from looking at her bare chest, but it was all he wanted to do. She looked as if she were about to say something to him, but she smiled instead. Her grin seemed to fill her entire face, revealing every tooth in her wide porcelainlike smile.

Arnold thought about what moment he could compare this one to but decided, for once, to abandon all thought, and dove in.

It was the first time during his journey that Arnold was able to forget everything and just be. Even though it was only for a few minutes, he badly needed it, and judging by the looks of relief on the travelers' faces, they needed it too. He'd forgotten what it was like to not worry about things so much. Lately, worrying was all he did. He was reminded how too much time spent focusing on one thing could weigh a person down.

They made it to the other side of the forest. Now the travelers would head south to find their fabled town of peach trees, while Arnold would continue east.

The travelers detailed their plans for the rest of their journey, but Arnold wasn't listening. All he could think about was abandoning his quest to travel with them instead, asking if he could tag along. More than anything, he didn't want to be alone again. The brief comfort of their company made him terrified to be without it. It wouldn't be so bad to walk away now, he thought, now that he had friends he could trust.

They hugged one another other goodbye and Arnold held his hug with Charlotte an extra second longer and she giggled. He thanked them for their help and they thanked him for the company. Arnold revealed a set of plastic containers from the Tower, large and small. He told them to use the containers to collect as many peaches as they could carry.

With that, Arnold watched the three turn south toward the grassy plains. He wanted so badly to call out to them, to chase them down and plead to join their group. But their journey ended at the town of peach trees. When they were done and returned home, Arnold would be alone again. The thought put a giant lump in his throat. He bit his tongue and swallowed, watching them fade into the distance.

He kicked up the brake and pushed the Tower forward again. Even made lighter by his gift to the travelers, the Tower felt heavier than it ever had before.

A few days after he'd said goodbye to Charlotte and her friends, Arnold started thinking more about time.

Since he had left home, he found that time was no longer something he had to worry about. This was another first for him. It didn't matter how long it took for him to get to his next destination, because whenever he arrived, whether it was night or day, he was always on time. Arnold laughed at the thought. He was habitually tardy, and over the years the weight of that had piled high. It became part of him, like some giant growth his parents kept asking about.

"You should really take care of that."

"When is it going to get better?"

"I guess you'll just have it forever."

Having them tell him over and over how bad of a problem it was never did anything to fix it. If anything, it made him want to do less about it. But on this journey with the Tower, there was no such thing as being late.

These thoughts were all triggered by a drifter who passed him, a man who had just completed a personal rite of passage. Where he was from, every male of age had to complete one in order to be deemed worthy of his bride and be accepted into her family.

The man looked like hell. He was pale, and dirty, his clothes ripped and stained from what looked like years of traveling. He asked Arnold for water, and while Arnold fetched the man some, he took notice of a watch on Arnold's wrist and became upset.

"Please, no. Take that off," the man begged.

Arnold looked at him, confused.

"You don't need it," the man said.

"Why not?"

The man told Arnold his story.

As his rite of passage demanded, the man was to travel to the home of a musical master, somewhere high up on a mountain. The man had to sit with the master and learn to play an ancient wooden instrument handed down by their indigenous ancestors. It was an unholy device, crafted to reach a specific octave obtained by making a long, low humming sound. The instrument was nearly impossible to play, but his ancestors had mastered it long ago and so he needed to as well.

To play the instrument, he first had to learn how to make the sound. The man, as most people who had gone through this rite of passage before, was ill prepared for the task. He had only brought the clothes on his back and a day's worth of food, thinking it wouldn't take longer than that day.

But he was wrong. A day turned into a week and a week turned into months. The man became gripped with frustration and grief at his inability to master the instrument. After a while, he was spending more time looking at his watch than he was practicing and learning. He counted every second he'd been away from home. Eventually the time consumed him completely.

One day, the master came to him with a request. He begged the man to throw the watch away and completely devote his mind, body, and soul to learning the sound and learning the instrument. The man could not do it.

"Let go," the master explained. "You must let go of time as something that pulls you apart and instead view it as a tool to make yourself stronger. It is what you create in time, not how much goes by, that matters."

"I don't believe that," the man said to the master.

"Then you will live the rest of your days in agony as a slave to time," the master responded. "Long after you have learned the instrument and leave my home, you will have accomplished nothing."

A year passed. Then two. Then three.

The man still had not learned how to make the sound or play the instrument and could not return home to marry his bride-to-be. This was the law of his people, their tradition.

The man refused to eat or sleep. His hair had grown long and curly, his beard mangled and rough. The skin around his eyes sagged. His ribs poked the surface of his skin. One night while lying on his cot, the man turned onto his side and let his arm hang over the edge. The ring he and his bride-to-be had worn as promises of their love to each other slid off his finger. He watched it, lying still as it hit the ground with a ping that reverberated through his skull.

He bent over and picked the ring up, staring at it for a moment. Then he threw it at the cave wall and frantically took off his watch and slammed it against the ground. Over and over again he struck it until it cracked, until it shattered. He hit it with fists clenched, scraping the skin off his knuckles until they bled and he wept.

The master appeared and presented the instrument. He placed it at the man's feet, saying nothing, and left him alone. Free from the bindings of time, the man had no choice but to learn. Time no longer held him captive, and with that understanding, he was finally able to do what he had to.

Now on his journey back home, he had spotted Arnold.

"You don't need it," the man repeated. He grabbed hold of Arnold's wrist and pointed to his watch. "This thing will rule you if you let it!"

He tried to wrestle the watch off Arnold's wrist, but Arnold pushed him away.

"Hey!" he yelled at him. "Back off!"

The man did. "I'm sorry . . . I just don't want you to make the same mistake as me."

And with that, the man shambled off toward his destination.

That night Arnold searched the Tower for anything that told time. He gathered up all the clocks and bargain-brand watches he owned, along with his mother's and father's high-end watches. They shone in the moonlight. He placed them into a pile beside the Tower and stared at them. He estimated their combined value at over twenty thousand dollars. He knew the watches well, especially the one his father wore to work every day. It was the kind of watch men in suits wore to business meetings while they tossed numbers at one another over steak and brandy. Mr. Blue had saved up for it for years, even forgoing renovations to the house to get it sooner. It had been a staple of Mr. Blue's wardrobe.

Arnold climbed up into the perch and pulled the hammer out from the toolbox. He twirled it in his palm and kneeled down beside the pile, ready to strike.

Then he froze. Something came over him. He stood up and tossed the hammer back into the perch and stared at the pile of clocks and watches. He gave it a nod and then walked to the Tower and kicked back the brake, pushing it forward.

He decided that time would no longer be his enemy, so he would not destroy it. Instead he would leave it behind, to find peace in his past. More important, Arnold had somewhere to be, and he was going to make it there on time.

The sound of music permeated the air as he reached the summit of a grassy hill. He hadn't heard music since he'd left the town of great wheels. He pushed the Tower into a soft notch in the grass and kicked out the brake. He stood next to the Tower, hands on his hips, looking down at the meadow below.

There was a village. Wooden huts were strewn about, with cobbled roads connecting them from door to door. From a distance, he made out a cluster of people centered in one area, moving like ants gathering food. Anxiety sent his stomach in a twirl at the thought of seeing new faces. But he took a deep breath, kicked in the brake again, and made his way down.

As he descended, the hill became rocky, making the Tower shake wildly. Arnold slowed to a crawl, carefully making sure to inch the wheels between each rock. Far from any repair shop, damaging the Tower was the last thing he could afford.

As he got closer, he was startled by an old bearded man who was urinating behind a boulder. The man noticed him, turning his head toward Arnold mid-stream, surprised. The bearded man's expression quickly turned into that of delight, however, as he zipped up his fly and danced toward Arnold, a big smile on his face. He grunted with every step and got right up next to Arnold, engulfing him in a tight hug.

"Whoa-ho!" Arnold said as air escaped his lungs.

The bearded man made his way around the other side of the Tower with a fit of grunts and flashy hand gestures. Arnold waved his hands to suggest he was fine, but the happy bearded man heard none of it as he started to lift the Tower up and pull it in the direction of the town.

"Oh no, I'm fine, thank you," Arnold pleaded to the bearded man. He replied in a language Arnold didn't understand.

Arnold quickly grabbed hold of the cart and picked it up, following the bearded man against his will. Another rush of anxiety flooded his heart and his limbs. It made him weak. The cheerful music got louder now as he was led to its source.

Before he could realize what was going on, Arnold found himself in the middle of a town square. It was filled from corner to corner with people dancing, singing, and playing music—children chasing one another, dogs barking at feverish feet. It was like something out of a fairy tale, where people danced in the streets to celebrate the end of an evil king's reign or the return of an epic war hero.

The bearded man stopped near a stone bench and dropped the Tower. Arnold's hands were red from hanging on to it for so long, but the relief was short-lived as the bearded man grabbed Arnold's arms and pulled him toward the crowd. His feet immediately turned to stone and he resisted the man. Dancing was the last thing he wanted to do.

He remembered his high school dances, where he would stand on the edge of the dance floor, filled with shame and envy as his classmates danced with ease. He remembered birthday parties and ceremonies, glued to his chair. While others danced, he sat and watched waiters change plates and deliver the next course. He always had the first pick. And like knotting a tie or buttoning a shirt, he would slip on his cement shoes as friends and family alike would attempt to drag him out of his seat.

But Arnold's resistance against the bearded man didn't last long. As if on cue, two large women came up behind Arnold and pushed him forward, lifting him off the ground. It was too much for the cement shoes to resist. He sprang forward into the crowd and joined a circle of dancers. An overwhelming shame poured over him. He felt the burning heat of being under a magnifying glass. All he could do was pace awkwardly in place and pray for some catastrophe to strike down all the musicians so there would be no more music to dance to.

But it never came, and the people around him continued to dance and smile. Men clapped to the rhythm of the music, some spinning in circles, some tapping their feet. A little boy ran into the middle of Arnold's circle and started dancing alone. The bearded man rushed in and spun the boy around. The dancing of the crowd was an entity all on its own, a sum of everyone and everything. It wasn't about Arnold, an outsider, joining in. It wasn't about who could dance or who could sing. It was about the rhythm, the music.

And, for the first time, he was able to let go. He let a smile take over his face while his feet gained traction. It was a motion he'd never attempted before, yet it felt familiar to him. The dancer lying dormant inside had just taken his first breath and continued to dance for what seemed like hours.

Arnold found a moment to slip away. He was sweaty and exhausted from all the dancing and needed a place to rest. He was also beginning to feel like he had overstayed his welcome at the village. That was a nasty habit of his: feeling unwanted in a place unless told otherwise. Feeling down on himself, he decided to press on and keep heading east. The high noon sun would soon begin to move across the sky.

Arnold dug through the Tower and pulled out an acoustic guitar, his acoustic guitar. It was a black six-string with a leather shoulder strap and a slot taped on the back to hold picks. A thick layer of dust covered it. He sat down on the plank and blew the dust away, watching it scatter in the sun's rays. He plucked a few strings. It was horribly out of tune; he hadn't played it in years. It was a hobby he had neglected after it failed to bring him any happiness.

He stood up and leaned the guitar against a rock, facing the village.

Someone will come out here eventually, he thought to himself.

Then he kicked in the brake and continued east again.

When Arnold was in school, he learned of great mountains in the east. Heading toward Kingdom meant he would have to scale those mountains eventually, something he wasn't prepared for. The ones he read about were over a thousand miles away from home, but as he approached the foot of the mountain in front of him, he couldn't help but think these were the ones from his books.

In any case, the rocky terrain made traveling difficult again. It slowed his pace significantly, and pushing the Tower became a test of patience. Every few feet he had to stop and lift the Tower up over a boulder or clear the path ahead of rocks and debris. The Tower had become an anchor Arnold had to drag along the bottom of the sea.

The mountain was steep. As he approached a summit, he pushed the Tower up with his legs, leaning his shoulder into the cart for leverage. He got it up and over, then stopped to catch his breath, kicking around loose rocks that littered the ground.

There was a depression in the surface, a square hole, about as wide as the cart, made of concrete and filled with tiny rocks. He wheeled the Tower there and squatted down next to it, digging his hand into the gravel. It seemed to go very deep.

He stood up, stroking his chin, and dipped a toe inside to reach for the bottom.

Nothing.

He went in farther, up past his ankle, leaning forward on his foot. His toe tapped against a hard surface. Without warning, the ground beneath him opened up and Arnold fell down onto his hands as his leg sunk into the hole. He flailed his leg around but felt nothing, and it sent a rush of terror through him.

The mountain was hollow beneath him.

He tried to pull himself up, forcing his leg out, but the ground around him started to crack as he struggled, like a thin sheet of ice over a river. He reached for the cart and pulled it toward him as a counterweight. The brake buckled against the surface of the mountain as he struggled to lift himself up. Puffs of dust burst from the cracks in the ground. They inched closer toward him, as if the ground were beginning to collapse under his weight.

He lay perfectly still, hoping the ground would hold while he formulated a plan. He turned slightly, attempting to twist his leg out rather than use sheer force. He pulled up part of his thigh, and a piece of the ground around his leg fissured as the rocks began to funnel downward, like water through a drain.

Through the crack, a brilliant beam of yellow light shot up at his face and blinded him. He shielded his eyes with his hand before slowly moving it away. He looked down in awe.

Something was below him—inside the mountain. He leaned in, trying to get a better look at it. The pivot caused the ground below him to give entirely. In a flash, he and the Tower fell through.

The brilliant yellow light consumed them as they plummeted through the crust of the earth in a free fall.

"Watch your father," Mrs. Blue said, her face glued to this month's fashion magazine. "Learn something from him. One day you'll have a family and you'll need to take care of them."

Mr. Blue was behind the living room TV, messing with the wiring. Arnold sat on the carpet, watching as tools were strewn about. Mrs. Blue sat behind them on the couch, casually thumbing through pages. The light from the Sunday sky beamed down on Arnold through the skylight overhead. He watched the dust particles dance in the light, thousands of microscopic dots that blocked out his father.

"Hand me that flat-head," Mr. Blue said, his voice muffled behind the television.

Instant hesitation. Arnold reached for the flat-head but pulled back. He reached instead for the Phillips-head screwdriver and handed it to his father.

"Arnold, I said the flat-head. Does this look like a flat-head to you? Use your brain."

"Sorry."

Arnold quickly scrambled back to his first choice and placed it in his father's hand. Mr. Blue said nothing.

Mrs. Blue flipped another page and said nothing as well, only throwing a concerned glance at her son, one that said, *You have a long way to go to become a real man.*

On the carpet next to the television were four screws that Mr. Blue had taken out to fix a broken outlet. Arnold picked them up, arranging them neatly on the table next to his father. It was all he could think to do.

He stared again at the dancing dust caught in the sunlight. Then a cloud rolled in and they disappeared.

7

ABANDONMENT

The gentle heat of the fire coaxed Arnold back to reality. The crackling of wood and the subtle aroma of smoke wafted through the air, awakening his senses as he came to. He was in a dimly lit cave, the only light a fire burning five feet away. Two thick logs rested on top of a pile of embers, other charred logs that had nearly burned to ash. He was lying on his back. As he opened his eyes, he attempted to lift himself up onto his elbows but was stopped abruptly by a viciously sharp pain in his left leg. He yelled, wincing in pain as he slowly lifted his neck and looked down at his leg.

His ankle was in some kind of wooden contraption. Two broad pieces of wood sandwiched it, with a rag underneath his heel to keep it suspended, and thin, flexible branches of wood intertwined to keep the bigger pieces in place. It was some kind of makeshift splint. The pain twisted around his foot and ankle, making it hard to pinpoint its exact source. He surmised that his foot was broken. It certainly felt that way.

He tried again to lift himself, but every motion brought him to the verge of tears. Instead he lay back down, trying his best to remain motionless and let the pain subside. He swiveled his head to check his surroundings.

The Tower was nowhere in sight.

He tried to piece together what he could remember before everything went dark. He'd fallen through the surface of a mountain and plummeted toward a yellow light, and now he was here, in this cave.

It sounded ridiculous in his head.

How long have I been out?

He looked down at his leg again. The pain distracted him from any more thoughts. He closed his eyes for a moment to relax, but they quickly became heavy and he passed out.

After some time Arnold woke up again. Through glazed eyes he looked over to the fire and saw that another pair of logs had been placed on top of the last two, which were now close to ash. He tried again to lift himself up, this time using only his upper body. Doing so hurt much less. Arnold dragged himself backward and up against the cave wall. The fire roared in front of him, and he saw a pale light leading to a tunnel that exited the cave. It was the only exit he could see.

He was able to better examine his leg from this angle. His foot was swollen and deep purple; just looking at it shot pain through his body. He closed his eyes, waiting to wake up again.

Coming from the mouth of the tunnel he heard scratching and the patter of feet. The ground was damp and it stuck to the soles of the prowler's feet with every step. Arnold panicked, thinking that he should slide back into his sleeping position. But he was sore. His whole body was in pain. He sat there as the footsteps grew louder. A shadow on the wall emerged. It turned the corner to reveal its owner, and Arnold felt his chest tighten.

A creature appeared before him, dragging two logs of wood, one in each hand. Upon seeing Arnold awake, it stopped just behind the ring of light cast from the fire and then placed the logs on the ground.

In the darkness the creature stood without a word, its beady yellow eyes staring at Arnold.

"Are you real?" Arnold asked, his voice echoing in the cave.

The creature remained silent. Arnold cleared his throat and the creature's ears perked up, like an animal's in the wild. It stepped into the light and Arnold saw it more clearly.

The creature stood before him, covered in brown and green scales, with a long jaw and a large head that looked like a stone sculpture. Its ears, still perked straight up near the top of its head, were also covered in scales. It wore a cloth robe, not unlike the ones worn by the people of the white city. It hung loosely over one shoulder and around its waist, draping down to its ankles. The creature resembled a kind of reptile that Arnold thought may have been a man at some point.

The creature's presence frightened Arnold, made his heart beat faster. He moved closer and kneeled next to Arnold's foot, examining it. Arnold noticed the creature had a horn the size of a tennis ball protruding from his head. The growth was wide and flat, but unmistakably a horn, and a pattern of scars covered one side of his face, like something had attacked him long ago. The creature placed his hands—five long, scaly fingers with sharp nails—around the wooden contraption. Pulling out one of the branches that kept the splint in place, he presented it to Arnold, who took it cautiously and looked back at the creature, confused. He pointed first to his mouth and then to Arnold's.

"You want me to eat this?" Arnold asked.

The creature continued pointing to Arnold's mouth. Arnold opened it and mimicked placing the branch in between his teeth. The creature nodded and made a clamping motion with his hand. Arnold reluctantly placed the stick between his teeth.

"Like thith? Am I doing thith ri—"

But before he could finish his sentence, the creature yanked at Arnold's ankle and twisted it. With a haunting snap that echoed through the cave, Arnold's anklebone popped back into place. He screamed, biting the stick hard until his eyes welled with tears and his face turned red.

The creature started massaging his calf, but Arnold shooed him away. The pain was too much. He fell over onto his side and curled into a ball. He lay there as the pain thumped in his ankle, and then he passed out again.

Somewhere between being awake and dreaming, he heard the sound of more logs being tossed onto the fire. The creature sat opposite him, sharpening some kind of tool. Arnold could still feel his beady yellow eyes beating down on him, and continued to feel them as he fell back into a dream.

He woke up again, this time just outside the mouth of the cave. A field with grass eight feet high towered in front of him. The air was stagnant, yet cool. Nothing moved.

He looked down at his ankle. It was significantly more swollen now. He felt like it was going to explode at any minute. His injury scared him, and not knowing the extent of it scared him even more.

From the corner of his eye the creature reappeared, wiping his hands with a dirty rag.

"Hello," said Arnold, attempting to talk to him again.

He remained silent.

"Do you speak?"

The creature stood before him. "Y-e-e-e-e-s-s-s," he sounded out slowly.

"Great," Arnold said, wincing. He rubbed his leg. "What happened to me?"

The creature spread his hands apart. "Broken." Then he interlocked his fingers. "I fix."

"Well, thank you," Arnold said, nodding.

The creature went back inside the cave. Arnold looked up at the sky. It was bright yellow, and it made his eyes hurt looking at it for more than a few seconds. He recognized the color—the same yellow that had blinded him when he'd fallen through the surface of the mountain.

The creature came back outside shortly after, carrying a blanket, which he then wrapped around Arnold. He examined the creature, as he was closer now. There were rings around the base of his horn, like the rings on a tree trunk.

"What's your name?"

The creature pulled back and pointed to the sky.

"Sky? Your name is sky?"

He shook his head and continued to point.

"Light? Sun?"

He shook his head again. "I . . . am Moon."

"Moon? Your name is Moon?"

He nodded.

"Okay, Moon . . . where am I? What is this place?"

Moon paid no attention to Arnold's questions and spread out the blanket down to Arnold's knee.

"How did I break my foot?"

Moon shook his head once more and wagged his finger, pointing to Arnold's ankle. He gingerly wrapped his fingers around it.

"My ankle? I broke my ankle?"

He nodded.

Arnold drew out a long sigh. "Was there anything else when you found me?"

Moon said nothing.

"I had stuff with me. It was tall and inside a . . . cart."

Moon stood up and walked around the side of the cave and out of sight.

"Hey! Where are you going? I—I can't move. I can't follow you."

Moments later Moon returned and presented to Arnold two wheels—the Tower's wheels. They were completely busted.

"What about the rest of it?"

Moon dropped his head.

"Tell me!" Arnold said, raising his voice. The tension in his muscles made his body ache.

Moon shook his head. "Broken . . ."

Arnold held the wheels tightly in his hands. The bent metal and limp rubber made them hard to hold.

"Take me to it," he demanded. "I want to see it."

Moon backed away, retreating into the cave.

Arnold took what was left of the wheels and grinded them into the dirt until they were caked with mud. He left the wheels there and leaned his head back against the cave wall, looking at the field in front of him. The tall grass stood at attention, as if it were staring at him. In this strange place, where the Tower was gone and he was unable to move, Arnold felt powerless. He was broken.

Three weeks went by. Arnold's clothes, tattered from his fall, were now dirty and brown, his hair filthy with even more grease and dirt. Every morning Moon helped him hobble to the mouth of the cave, and let him sit there while he disappeared for the day. Then he would return hours later with food and they would eat by the fire inside the cave. Arnold examined Moon every chance he could get, studying his complexities. Each passing day, his horn grew smaller, indicated by a new ring at its base. Moon rarely spoke and when he did, he seemed to struggle with every syllable. It discouraged Arnold from asking him many questions, and in time, they began to mirror each other. Soon the only sounds inside the cave were the crackling fire and the chewing of nuts and berries.

Moon carried around an obvious melancholy. Sadness lingered in his every step, his every motion. Arnold speculated that the man Moon used to be before he became the scaly creature he was now was someone entirely different. Something significant had happened to him, and he carried the consequences of that every minute, every day.

One day when Moon had left him outside, Arnold decided to venture farther out. Enough time had passed, and he was able to walk without help. The swelling in his ankle had gone down significantly, and now he dealt with tenderness and bruising. He approached the tall grass and tried to look through the motionless blades. Slowly, he pushed the grass aside and limped through. He imagined they would part, like wading through a field of cornstalks, but the blades cracked and crunched as he stepped over them, crumbling almost instantly. They were brittle, like dead leaves in the winter. The lack of natural sun had turned them into hollow shells, unable to bend and sway. He thought he may have been the first person to ever step foot here.

Still he continued, limping through the grass, pushing patches to the side. The field seemed to go on forever.

Finally he stopped to catch his breath and rest his ankle. He matted a circle around him and sat down. He gently rubbed the area around his wounded ankle. It pulsed as blood rushed through. He grabbed a handful of grass and tore it from the ground. It cracked and snapped into little pieces in his hand. He blew on the fragments, watching them float up into the air. Even with no wind to carry them, the grass somehow was light enough to float.

His eyes followed the pieces into the sky and that was when he saw it. Back toward the mouth of the cave, above where he had spent the last three weeks, was a city. Some two hundred feet above the cave opening, in the mountains, were rows of walls and windows, homes carved into the rock face touching the east and west ends as far as he could see. There were huge caverns dug into the mountain wall where the city extended deeper and deeper.

"Why was Moon keeping this from me?" Arnold asked himself.

If there's a city, there have to be people. And if there're people . . .

" . . . they have to know where we are," Arnold finished out loud.

Arnold limped back toward the cave, determined to find a way into the city. When he returned, Moon was nowhere to be found. He made it inside the cave and saw that the fire was down to embers. Moon would return soon.

Back outside, he walked along the side of the mountain, looking for a way up. After a few minutes he came across a small indent in the wall with a gap wide enough for him to squeeze through. On the other side, it opened up into a larger crevice where a wooden ladder pressed against the mountain, laced together with thick rope. He stood next to it and looked up. It seemed to go on forever, with nothing but the ladder to hang on to. It was a sheer cliff. Arnold grabbed hold of one of the rungs and propped his foot up. He lifted himself slowly, but the gravity painfully weighed on his ankle. He lowered himself back onto the ground and looked up.

"You need to get up there," he whispered to himself.

He grabbed the ladder and lifted himself again, this time hopping onto the rung. Like ripping off a bandage, the pain was intense but quick.

If he did it slowly, he could hop from one rung to the next and reach the top. He kept both hands on one rung at a time and lifted himself up step by step.

Arnold had climbed ten feet up the ladder when he had to stop to catch his breath. After that he had to pause every few rungs to rest his arms. The ladder swayed more with each hop he took. Sweat started to dot his hairline. The stagnant air did nothing to cool him down.

Higher up now, he realized that he hadn't really anticipated how great of a climb it was to reach the city. He felt like a madman to attempt such a thing, but he hadn't been thinking clearly as of late. He was still riddled with guilt and anguish over the loss of the Tower.

He pressed on though.

His resolve to reach the surface was greater than his fear of falling.

Up thirty feet.

Up forty feet.

Arnold's arms burned with every step and the ladder only swayed more wildly. The higher he got, the longer he had to wait for the ladder to stop moving.

He was a quarter of the way to the top now. Fifty feet. He looked down for a brief moment but quickly shut his eyes to block out the dizzying height. He hugged the ladder tightly between his arms. The fear of falling began to seep in again and now overshadowed his resolve. It made his legs weak.

Without the Tower to rely on, it was just him, alone in the air. The only thing he could rely on now was the will to live.

He opened his eyes again and looked up. The city was closer now. He could just make out the protruding white stone walls.

"You can do this," he told himself.

He continued to climb.

Up one hundred feet.

Up one hundred and fifty feet.

Finally he made it to the top.

He reached for the edge of the cliff face, grabbing on to two anchored posts, and lifted himself up. He rolled onto the ground and into a vegetable garden, gasping for air, sweat trickling down to his lower back. He got up onto his knees and surveyed the garden. A low stone fence bordered it, serving to keep people from running off the edge of the cliff. He stood up and leaned against the fence, looking around for any signs of life, still catching his breath. It was eerily quiet—the still air, the absence of wildlife, of chatter. It all added to the strangeness of everything.

The garden was filled with patches of purple lilies, and they stood out against the stark white building next to it. It was crudely made, like a relic from the Stone Age, riddled with cracks and irregular bumps, the marks of a handmade home. But there was a certain charm to it. He felt an odd, peaceful calm, as if the home and garden had belonged to him in a different life.

He walked up to the building and looked around, peeking into a window, which was nothing more than a hole cut into the stone. The same went for the front door. It enticed him to enter, but the whole situation felt wrong. He had to find someone first.

He followed a stone path inside the garden to a dirt path in front of the stone hut. There were no gates, just an opening in the fence. The lilies continued past the garden and had changed to yellow, arranged in long rows that marked walking paths down the road as far as he could see. He followed them, keeping his head on a swivel. He wanted to spot someone before they spotted him. If they looked anything like Moon, he imagined they might be startled to see him. He didn't want to be surprised.

Just then, a loud bell rang in the distance. It was low and deep and shook the ground. Arnold crouched down out of fear. The sound rang out for some time, and he looked around to see if anything had changed. After a minute the sound dissipated, and Arnold felt an uneasy air around him. It was the feeling of being watched. He got to his feet and hopped to another stone hut close by.

He had just made it behind the house when a row of creatures emerged from a flat-roofed building farther down the path. They walked single file, in complete silence. Then, one by one, as the paths branched off, they changed course and headed off in different directions. He watched them through a row of lilies, waiting for the right time to reveal himself. He wanted to handle the situation delicately and approach one of the creatures alone.

He waited for what seemed like an eternity.

Eventually they all disappeared and Arnold stood up. The moment had passed him by and he was immediately disappointed in himself for not approaching one of the creatures.

He turned around to head back toward the first hut but was suddenly met by the long face of another scaly creature. It stared at him, without a sound.

"Uh, h-hello. Hi," he said to the creature.

"H-e-e-e-l-l-o-o-o," he sounded out slowly, bowing his head slightly.

"I hope I didn't alarm you," Arnold said.

The creature bowed his head again.

"Can you tell me where I am? I'm . . . not sure what's going on." He felt crazy for asking, but to his surprise, the creature nodded.

He turned to walk away, signaling with two fingers for Arnold to follow. He led him inside the hut they were standing outside of.

The interior was drab and mostly empty. The walls were covered in foreign shapes and patterns of every color. The yellow light shone through the windows, illuminating the entire home. The walls glistened and glowed, seeming to move as he did. Even as he got closer to them, the shapes and patterns were nothing but scribbles to him, something akin to cave drawings but with brighter colors and more contoured lines. Arnold reached for the ceiling, and was able to place his palms flat on the cool stone.

The creature made for the back of the hut, somewhere out of sight, and Arnold followed. It was sitting in the middle of the floor in what appeared to be the bedroom, with a long, thin rug and a pillow at one end.

Arnold had never been so overwhelmed by so little before. Wall writings, holes for doors and windows, a wooden ladder as an entrance to the city, flowers that lined the streets . . . they were indications of an open, communal society. There were no doors to open, no shaded windows to hide secrets behind. It was all unfamiliar to Arnold, as he had spent most of his life feigning ignorance to what was going on behind the closed doors of his own home.

The creature signaled Arnold to come over, and so he sat down in front of him.

"I . . . am Ilium. You . . . are here for a reason," the creature said, struggling to speak.

"What? What do you mean?"

"You . . . are here . . . to . . . be fixed," Ilium replied.

"Fixed?"

"Yes. You . . . are broken . . . like all . . . who come here."

Arnold didn't know what to make of Ilium's cryptic words. "Oh, you mean because of my limp?" He pointed to his foot. "I broke my ankle a few weeks ago, but it's better now."

"Still . . . broken," Ilium replied, ignoring Arnold's comment.

"I'm not sure what you mean. I'm not broken. I just . . . lost something of mine. Something . . . important."

"You . . . are not . . . *lost.*"

"I know. It's not me I'm talking about."

"Yes . . . it is."

Arnold tried to change the subject. "Can you tell me where I am?"

"Where you need . . . to be."

Arnold rubbed the back of his head and neck. Ilium was just like Moon in that nothing he said was straightforward. They spoke as if it were up to Arnold to figure out their meaning for himself.

Ilium reached under the pillow on his bed and pulled out a leather-bound book dyed a deep burgundy. He handed the book to Arnold. There was no text on either cover, and when Arnold opened it, it was filled with drawings. Ilium turned it to a specific page and made a gesture, suggesting for Arnold to flip through the pages on his own.

The book told a visual story of the creature' history. It started with giant, empty fields and a few creatures tending to those fields with gardening tools. Flowers appeared, much like the lilies in the city, and more creatures came to build shelters at the base of a mountain.

He turned the page.

The population doubled in size. The creatures built more homes and had families. They began preaching of settlements from far away that were looking to bring war into their community.

He turned the page again and grimaced at the imagery.

Fire. Blood. Chaos. Buildings set ablaze. Creatures fleeing their homes. A foreign army had marched in, just as the creatures had predicted, trampling buildings and killing villagers.

He hesitated to turn the page, but Ilium nodded.

The bloodshed continued as some of the villagers started to retaliate. They clawed at the flesh of the men and bit them, sinking their nails and teeth into their necks and arms. The men began to flee. The surviving creatures stood over corpses lying in pools of blood.

He turned to the next page, where the village was empty, in ashes. The remaining population moved up the mountain, where they tried to recover from their losses. It was there that they discovered the secret of the mountain. It was hollow inside.

Here, they built a new city to hide from other civilizations who might incite war against their people. Then Arnold noticed something else. The population had begun to grow horns: short, flat horns. They were faint, but they were there.

He looked up at Ilium and noticed there was nothing on his forehead.

"You don't look like them."

"They . . . are the last . . . of the Settlers. They . . . made this place," Ilium said.

"So it's true where we are," said Arnold. "We're inside the mountain."

Ilium nodded.

"How do I get out of here?"

"You cannot leave . . . until you . . . are fixed."

Arnold closed the book, then looked down at his ankle. It was starting to ache again. Ilium stood up and took the book from him, placing it on a shelf near his bed.

"So once I'm better, you'll show me how to get back to the surface?"

Ilium turned to him. "It is . . . not up to . . . me. You must . . . be fixed."

He left the room. Arnold was alone now. It was quiet in Ilium's home, but the noise in his head smashed the silence with a hammer. He thought about McFulty and the town of great wheels, of the white city and the time he'd spent with Charlotte and her friends. It all seemed so long ago, and he couldn't help but feel like it was all for nothing. Now that the Tower was gone, gone with it was his chance of ever reaching Kingdom. He would never be able to make it there alone.

Maybe losing it is a sign, he thought. *Maybe it was supposed to get me here instead. Maybe this is Kingdom.*

Arnold leaned on the idea that perhaps Kingdom was different for each individual who pursued it. Maybe Kingdom was just an ideology. Maybe it could exist anywhere. McFulty wasn't even sure himself, and he was the one who had suggested it.

There was no way to know, and all the possibilities of what and where Kingdom could be ate at him.

He shook his head, falling too deep into his own mind. He tried to look at the facts.

The Tower was gone and he wasn't.

If he had to prepare for a future without the Tower, spending some time here to recover and plan out his next move wouldn't be so bad. It didn't look like he had much of a choice anyway. But maybe it was what he needed: a situation that forced him in a direction. That feeling was comfortable to him.

Ilium returned shortly, carrying a robe much like the one he had on. He signaled for Arnold to wear it.

"You . . . can stay . . . with me . . . until . . . you are fixed."

Arnold rubbed the fabric between his thumb and index finger.

"Okay, but I'll only stay for a few days . . . until I'm ready to leave," Arnold said. Ilium nodded.

Kingdom. The Tower. Home.

Maybe it was okay to let go. Maybe it was fine to have tried and failed, just like all the times before. Nobody had to know that he didn't keep going. And as long as the Tower was gone, nobody ever would.

After two weeks in the mountain city, Arnold learned that there were no clear distinctions between day or night. Time seemed to move indefinitely, bathed in a perpetual light that, at most, dimmed to a twilight. The unnatural yellow light seemed to come from everywhere and nowhere, as if it permeated through holes in the surface, like spotlights. It was one of many abnormalities he had come to notice.

Living with Ilium proved to be much easier than he had expected. It didn't take long for Arnold to get comfortable with his new accommodations, and it was made easier by how accepting the creatures were. He learned that he was not the first outsider to find their secret city, and that all who had come before him had come broken too. When they were fixed, they left of their own will. The thought that he could leave whenever he wanted comforted him, but it also seduced him to take his time.

Life without the Tower felt empty, but Ilium and his community helped to fill the void. Arnold was able to cope by distracting himself with whatever Ilium asked of him. In exchange for being allowed to live in his home, Ilium had Arnold go with him every morning to a large circular dirt field about an hour's walk away. There, they would tend to a garden that would sprout new lilies to eventually spread all over the city—watering, raking, and maintaining the field. Each day started off slow, as Arnold wasn't able to walk far without feeling pain in his ankle. But after a couple weeks, he was healed and able to put in a full day of work.

Arnold realized the day his leg was healed when Ilium approached him with a peculiar question. After a day of tending to the lily fields, Arnold and Ilium arrived home and began to unwind. Ilium approached a sitting Arnold with a damp towel. Arnold took it and wiped down his forehead.

"When . . . are you going . . . to fix?" Ilium sounded out.

Arnold wiped the back of his neck and looked up at Ilium. "What do you mean? My ankle is fine."

"No . . . fix." Ilium pointed to Arnold's chest.

Arnold looked down at his chest and rubbed it. "There's nothing else that needs fixing."

Ilium continued pointing at Arnold's chest, unfazed. Arnold let out a nervous laugh and got up, walking toward a makeshift cot that had been serving as his bed. He sat down on it.

"I don't know what you're talking about."

"If you want . . . to return . . . home . . . you need . . . to fix," Ilium said.

"I want to return to the surface. I never said home," Arnold replied defiantly. "Besides, I can leave whenever I want. You said that."

Ilium stepped closer to him. "No."

"No?"

"No. You . . . don't leave. You . . . don't want . . . to be fixed."

Arnold stood up again and scoffed at Ilium. "I don't know where this is coming from. I can leave whenever I want. You said when I'm fixed, I can go. I told you my ankle is fine."

He threw the towel down and stormed out of the room. If there had been a door to slam, he would have slammed it. Instead he exited Ilium's home, into the twilight, and made for a tall building near the edge of town.

The tall building had a larger entrance than any of the other buildings in the city, as it served as a meeting area for the creatures. Inside, six creatures circled a massive gong-like instrument, their heads down as if they were meditating. Arnold stood by the entrance, watching them. Then he walked in and took a seat near the back corner, a place where he could observe but not interfere. He leaned his head against the wall and closed his eyes, listening to the creaking of wood and the soft breathing of the creatures. He thought about what Ilium had been trying to tell him and why he thought Arnold wasn't fixed. He pulled his ankle over his knee and rubbed it with his hands.

I'm fixed, he thought. *I can leave.*

His eyes wandered. The murals on the walls showed parts of the creatures' history that he had read about in Ilium's book. But unlike in the book, these murals didn't show the violence of their past. The creatures didn't want to put their troubled history on display, the opposite of what Arnold had done with the Tower. He wondered if this was their way of ignoring their past or a way to move on from it. To him, it felt like hiding, and it was a feeling he was familiar with. In the time he had spent in the city, he had tried his best to forget all about the Tower. It felt like a life he had dreamed of rather than lived.

A thought dawned on him, and he remembered how McFulty had asked him what he was running from. At the time, Arnold had vehemently denied that he was running from anything and said that he was in fact heading toward something new.

Sitting by himself, in the corner of a room, with a tribe of creatures he knew little about, in a city hidden from the world, he realized he was wrong. It was never home he was running from. And now it wasn't the Tower he was running from.

Suddenly the creatures surrounding the massive gong-like instrument each picked up a mallet from a stack on the ground and struck the instrument in unison, sending a low, reverberating hum into the ground. The vibration shook Arnold out of his head. Whatever the creatures were doing seemed to be coming to a close. He quickly stood up and headed outside. He could still feel the vibration under his feet.

He headed back to Ilium's home.

On his way, he spotted one creature walking by itself. Something told him to get a closer look at it, so he walked on a parallel path and sped up. He followed it toward the edge of the city, which overlooked the valley at the base of the mountain. Arnold followed the creature for as long as he could, taking cover behind fences and houses, getting as close as possible. As the creature turned a corner, Arnold saw that it had a fully grown horn on its forehead, flat and wide and protruding farther than any he'd seen before.

Just as quickly as he had seen it, the creature disappeared from view. Arnold backed off and shook his head, deciding once again to return to Ilium's home. The sky had turned amber, signaling nightfall in the city.

He returned home to find Ilium asleep. There were so many things he wanted to tell the creature, things he wanted to ask him, about the Tower, about himself, about what needed to happen so he could be fixed. He wanted to wake Ilium up and talk about it all.

He walked over to his cot and lay down, letting his desire to move on fade away.

A month went by. After weeks of tending to the lily gardens, Arnold was able to walk to and from the garden every day, and work by himself. The flowers had grown substantially since his first day, to over three feet tall. The large circular patch of dirt was now completely covered in these flowers, and every day Arnold tended to them, watering them and waiting for the first ones to bloom. Once they were all ready, he would harvest them and plant them around the city so that they could join the thousands of flowers already lining the dirt roads and sidewalks.

One day, as Arnold sat among the flowers, staring up at the ceiling of the carved-out mountain, he caught the bloom of a white lily out of the corner of his eye. Six trumpet-shaped petals with a hint of green marked in the center of each one. He got up to his knees and put his nose into the flower, breathing in the sweet smell. It instantly reminded him of the bright orange leather bag that had fallen from the Tower, the one he had smelled on his first day away from home. At the time, he understood how that smell could have been so intoxicating, but after smelling the first breath of a brand-new flower, he questioned how anything man-made could rival something so pure.

He stood up and saw that even more bulbs had unfolded. Soon, the entire crop was blooming around him. The sweet smell permeated the air and bathed Arnold in their awakening.

He returned to the city to tell Ilium of the good news, and they walked back to the field together, ready to harvest their new yield.

Ilium stretched an arm out and gently grazed the petals of a flower. "Miracle . . ." he said.

"Huh?"

"Every flower . . . is . . . a miracle," Ilium said.

Arnold looked down at the flowers and grazed one with his fingers as well. "Why lilies?" he asked.

"Every lily . . . is different. An . . . identity. Name . . . bloom . . . color . . ." He looked at Arnold. "Just . . . like us. Like . . . you."

Arnold looked at Ilium now.

"We all . . . grow . . . at different times . . . and in . . . different ways," Ilium continued. "But every time . . . it is . . . a miracle."

Arnold looked away. He couldn't help but think of the Tower and how he missed it. Even though it was easier to try to move on and forget it, he knew he had a better chance at the future he needed, an opportunity to grow, with the Tower. Things were harder when it was around, but deep down he knew it was what he wanted.

"Let's start cutting these stems," Arnold said, sniffing, his nose suddenly congested.

Together they crouched in the dirt and started to root out the flowers, one by one. They worked in silence.

As the sky's amber color deepened, Arnold and Ilium returned home, carrying baskets filled with dozens of lilies. They set them just outside the hut's entrance and went in to sleep.

"I have to ask you something," Arnold said as Ilium prepared his bed. The creature nodded at him.

"These Settlers . . . ," he began. "The ones that have those horns. I've been wondering, why them and not you? Why do *they* have horns?"

Ilium closed his eyes and let out a sigh, as if he had answered this question many times before.

"The Settlers . . . paid a price."

"What do you mean?"

"To live . . . a life . . . of atonement."

"For what, protecting themselves?"

Ilium nodded again. "No deed . . . good . . . bad . . . is without . . . consequence. The Settlers . . . live . . . and die . . . in atonement."

Arnold looked into Ilium's beady yellow eyes.

"When I first woke up here, I was badly injured. But someone saved me, gave me shelter in his cave, one of these Settlers, I think. And he had a horn, only it seemed to be getting smaller and smaller."

Ilium appeared to be smiling out of the corner of his mouth. It was the first time Arnold had seen anything resembling a smile.

"He . . . was fixing . . . you."

Arnold raised an eyebrow. "Fixing me? Like, my ankle?"

"No. Fixing you," Ilium repeated, pointing to Arnold's chest.

Arnold looked out of the window at the amber sky. It seemed to swirl in the air like hot caramel.

Suddenly he knew what he had to do. "I have to go see something," he said to Ilium. Then he walked out of the room and into the twilight.

The sky cast a light on him and lit up the entire face of the city. He headed toward the garden of purple lilies, where the ladder rested on the edge of the cliff that fed into the canyon.

He neared the edge and dropped to his knees, digging his fingers into the dirt for leverage. The wind came and swept up his hair, pelting him with a swirl of dust. He shielded his eyes and then rubbed the dust out. In the valley below, down toward the base of the mountain, he looked for Moon.

But he was not there.

Instead he saw a ghost, a shadow of something he thought had been buried away. It jolted his brain, like an engine revving to life. Waves of suppressed emotions rushed in, churning his empty stomach. He felt like he had been woken up from a deep sleep and thrust back into a life he'd thought he could dream away forever.

It was the Tower.

He dug his knuckles into his eyes. A static field momentarily blinded him, but even after it dissipated, the Tower still stood. It looked up at him defiantly, challenging him to make his move. Arnold felt the urge to jump over the edge and finish what should have happened the day he'd fallen through the mountain's surface.

A figure appeared next to the Tower. It was Moon.

Arnold had a choice in front of him now. It stared him in the eyes, daring him from two hundred feet below. He dug his fingers deeper into the dirt and leaned farther over the ledge.

He wondered if a leap of faith was only true for something new. He wondered if a leap from this high would kill him.

8

BREAK DOWN

"Frederick! Frederick?"

No answer.

"Annie!"

Arnold's voice carried little weight through the damp wood of the forest. He listened for a response, but there was only the pitter-patter of rain. He threw up the hood of his bright yellow raincoat and kept moving.

He had been looking for Annie first, but was now looking for Frederick, too. After almost three hours of traveling deeper into the forest, he was starting to doubt he'd ever find them. He hoped to find Annie first. Finding her first would keep things from getting worse than they already were.

There was a hill in front of him, and he climbed it to get a better vantage point. The ground was wet, and his boots sunk deep into the mud with each step. The animals that had fled their homes made the quiet around him almost deafening.

The three hours alone in the damp forest felt longer than the ten days he had been living with Annie and Frederick. In that time, he quickly learned just how much Frederick really loved Annie. She was like his family. They went everywhere, did everything together. Frederick had even told Arnold that he wished she could live long enough that they could grow old together. He told him about his irrational fears of losing her, like that one day she would be kidnapped by an evil corporation because her DNA was the key to a billion-dollar antidote, or that she was a super-secret undercover agent and would leave him when activated. The fears were silly, but Arnold knew what lay beneath them: Frederick was preparing for the pain he would feel from losing someone again.

Frederick told Arnold stories of his home. A society obsessed with expanding their infrastructure led a determined charge to knock down the neighboring forest and excavate it for new buildings and factories. This forest, Frederick's home, was the last standing memory of his parents, who had been killed leading a revolt to stop the society's leaders from destroying everything. Ever since then, Frederick lived on his own, with Annie, in a cabin in the woods, keeping an eye on the machines that threatened to topple the rest of the forest at any moment. In his parents' absence, Frederick had taken matters into his own hands, leading a new wave of protests and public showings to stop the machine-obsessed society from doing more damage.

He even went so far as to disable machines in the dark of night, hoping to one day destroy the entire fleet.

Frederick had taken Arnold along on one of these missions. One night Arnold, Frederick, and Annie snuck into a parking lot where a huge bulldozer stood, holding its place until the morning, when it would begin excavating a new patch of land. Frederick clipped a hole in a fence surrounding the lot and the three of them slipped through, running with their heads down so as not to be spotted.

"Are you ready for this?" Frederick asked Arnold as they pressed up against the wall of a guard tower.

"I am," Arnold replied.

Truthfully, Arnold was ill prepared for the task. His mind was elsewhere: Kingdom, the Tower, and how much more time he would waste helping Frederick with his hopeless quest. He had already spent a week with him, and every day that went by seemed to pull him farther from his own goals.

Frederick handed Arnold a pair of hedge trimmers.

"You can do this," he said. "Make sure you cut enough so you puncture the rubber. That will ensure that the machines can't move. And try to keep the cuts hidden. The longer it takes for them to realize what's wrong, the better it is for us."

Us, Arnold thought.

Frederick grabbed Annie, and the two of them dashed toward the other end of the parking lot. Arnold snuck in the opposite direction, keeping an eye out for any guards. He approached a row of excavator mulchers, yellow behemoths with cranes armed to the teeth with a dozen sawblades. He crawled up next to one of the giant tires of the machine and opened the hedge trimmers around it. He tried to close them and cut through the tire, but the treading was too thick. He tried again, pushing the blades deeper into the rubber. The blades barely moved.

Just then, a light went on in the guard tower above him. Arnold circled the tires, out of view, and pressed his back up against the machine. He heard a commotion coming from the tower and clenched the trimmers against his chest.

What am I doing here? This isn't me. This isn't for Kingdom.

A door to the building opened and he heard two voices and then the creaking of the door closing.

Almost on impulse, Arnold threw the trimmers over the fence, into a tall field of grass. He got down onto his stomach and crawled underneath the excavator. He inched over a few paces before the collar of his shirt got caught on a sharp piece of metal.

"Oh no, don't do this," he whispered.

He kept crawling forward until his shirt stretched and a piece tore off and he was free. He heard the voices again and looked on from underneath the machine to see the two men talking to each other. They were dressed in navy uniforms. One of them had his hand leaning on a holster on his belt, a pistol inside it. Arnold waited for what seemed like an eternity before they separated and walked out of view.

He crawled out from underneath the machine and looked around for anyone else.

"Frederick!" he whispered.

There was no answer.

Arnold snuck around to the front of the machine and looked into the cockpit. On the floor, near the pedals, was a long metal chain. He grabbed it and brought it around the machine near the fence. There he wove the chain through the pipes underneath the machine in a dizzying mess and locked the chain around the fence.

He did the same for the machines next to him before making his way back toward the hole in the fence that Frederick had cut. There he waited for Frederick to return, thinking about the Tower. He feared that if any one found out that he was involved in Frederick's antics, they would go after him too.

"Arnold?" a voiced whispered.

Frederick had returned from his half of the mission.

"How did it go?" he asked Arnold.

Arnold gave him a thumbs up and exhaled.

"Where are the clippers?"

"I had to toss them."

"Ah, no worries," Frederick said, pulling Arnold in close by the shoulder. "This is going to be a big victory for us."

Frederick looked at Arnold's neck.

"What happened to your shirt?"

"It got caught on something."

"Good riddance. That's an ugly shirt anyways," Frederick said, laughing.

After their mission was deemed a success, the three went back to Frederick's cabin, where Frederick celebrated, laughing and telling stories of future victories. Arnold listened and chimed in when he could, fighting back a sinking feeling in the pit of his stomach.

Days later the steel machines came in the night. Startled and fearing for his life, Arnold jumped out of bed and sprinted for the Tower, parked just outside Frederick's cabin. The roar of the machine was so loud, it rattled the walls. Frederick also jumped out of bed, startled by Annie before anything else. She sprinted from room to room, barking in the darkness as they scrambled for the door. The clanking of the machine threatened to tear down the walls at any moment. Frederick picked Annie up and ran into the forest as Arnold pushed the Tower as fast as it could go.

It was dark and the forest was dense. Arnold hopped up to the front of the Tower and flicked on a lantern that was dangling off the handle of a broom. The light was dim, but it illuminated enough for them to carve a path to safety. They ran into the night until the whir of the machine was distant enough for them to catch their breaths. They looked back toward the white glow of the city behind them, a city of towering steel and metal, exposed pipes and grinding cogs. Arnold glanced over at Frederick, who looked on in disbelief as the machine absorbed his wooden home.

A blast fired off nearby and they both jumped. In the sudden shock, Annie leapt from Frederick's arms and ran off into the woods. Frederick called her name and chased after her. Arnold followed suit and ran after Frederick, begging him to slow down.

Now, hours later, the day broke, and Arnold had wandered deep into the forest, alone. There was no trace of Frederick or Annie anywhere.

Arnold made it to the top of the hill. It was high enough to see beyond the trees for a few dozen yards, but he couldn't see much. The overcast sky blended in with the gray city. He peered over to the side, where he'd left the Tower perched between two giant red oaks. If he was going to find Frederick and Annie, he needed to be mobile.

"Frederick!" he called out again. His voice carried a little farther, but there was still no answer. "Annie!"

He feared he had lost them both. In the distance he could see treetops disappearing one by one and he could still hear the distant hum of the machine. Soon the trees would be replaced with steel beams. He wondered if the only way to find his friends was to wait until the entire forest had been torn down.

Without the forest, his path to Kingdom would be much clearer too, but he couldn't just leave. If he had learned anything, it was to never abandon anyone. The Tower had taught him that.

He continued through the forest, listening acutely for any helpful sounds. It was quiet. The rain had stopped and his breath lingered in the air. A chill ran through him as he folded his arms and hugged his body for warmth.

"Frederick!"

His voice sounded foreign in the quiet forest, like an unfamiliar sound in a dark room.

It started to snow.

Arnold made his way back to the Tower and threw on an extra sweater. He sat down on the cold plank and curled into himself, breathing slowly. He thought about home, about snow days spent looking out his window while the neighbors built snowmen and snow angels. If he knew then how much colder things could get, he wouldn't have been so scared to join them. It all seemed so easy now.

But he wasn't giving up yet. Arnold stood and went around the side of the Tower to examine it. He looked over the updated frame of the cart. Moon had reinforced it with thick wooden boards to keep it from shaking and allow it to withstand more abuse. The wood was sanded and coated with a kind of protective layer against rain and dirt. On one of the boards was a word that he didn't recognize: *Libri*. Another letter next to the second *i* was faded beyond recognition. Arnold thought it might be a word from a language only the Settlers, like Moon, knew. Moon had also installed new wheels with reinforced plates to help the Tower push through snow and mud, moving both to the sides like a plow.

He began a search of the Tower's innards, looking for a whistle or something that could help him find Frederick and Annie. He found nothing, except for a lighter, the one his mother had used to light her cigarettes whenever she and Mr. Blue had gotten into screaming matches. He found the cigarette pack, too, and held it in his hand. He stared at it as thick snowflakes began to cover the lettering on the pack. He flicked off the snow and turned the pack upside down, shaking it until all the cigarettes fell out. He pushed them into a pile using his feet, then grabbed a few branches nearby. He pushed his thumb down on the lighter to strike the flint. It lit up, and he lit the pile on fire. He hoped the smell would waft far enough for Frederick and Annie to pick up. He hoped it would be foreign enough that they would come seeking it.

He walked a perimeter, continuing to call out their names, but to no avail. What seemed like hours passed. The smell of cigarettes had all but disappeared, and the forest was now completely covered in snow. Arnold was at a loss.

He made his way back to the hill and looked toward the steel city again. A row of trees was missing near the horizon, and the whir of the machines carried far into the distance. Soon the city's reach would expand to where he stood, and then out even farther.

Arnold told himself that Frederick would rebuild his home somewhere else and continue to live in peace with Annie.

"Nature always wins," Frederick had told Arnold. "And I intend to be on her side throughout."

Frederick's parents had spent their lives instilling in him their principles and the dangers of industrial expansion. They had given their lives fighting against it. The forest was more than just Fredrick's home now; it was his responsibility. Whatever Frederick could have been or should have been when his parents were still alive didn't matter anymore. This was his life.

Arnold wanted to believe everything would work out in the end.

He decided to make his way back toward the city, toward Frederick's cabin. Through the fresh blanket of snow, he rolled the Tower forward. Its reinforced wheels cut through with greater ease than he'd expected.

He made it back to the cabin. One corner of it was still standing. The dilapidated structure had been ripped open, chewed up by metal teeth. What used to be a roof and walls were now pulp. Arnold carefully stepped over the debris of wood and broken glass. The Tower rolled over a thin board, and a piece of glass crunched underneath it. He stepped back and lifted the wood up, revealing a framed photo of Frederick and his parents. On his lap sat Annie, when she was just a pup. Even though Frederick was tall and skinny, his cheeks were plump, like his baby fat had never gone away. His face seemed to be fighting with itself for space.

Arnold slipped the photo out, folded it, and placed it in his pocket. Something else was poking out from underneath the debris. He recognized the color. He pushed a slab of wood with his foot to reveal it and bent down to pick it up. It was a piece of Arnold's shirt.

He swallowed a lump in his throat and quickly placed the cloth in his other pocket, looking to see if anyone was around.

He heard what sounded like laughter not too far off. He parked the Tower under what was left of the cabin and walked outside, about thirty yards away. There was Frederick, on his knees, hunched over in the middle of a field of trees that had just been cultivated. Wide stumps and shredded wood littered the ground. He rocked back and forth while Arnold approached him cautiously. He leaned in just enough to see what he was hunching over. It was Annie. Frederick whispered to her as he was rocking.

"Frederick?" Arnold called out softly.

He made out the whispers now.

"I'm sorry. I'm sorry. I knew."

He repeated it again and again. Arnold wanted to sit down beside him and comfort him, but Frederick was beyond his help.

He backed up slowly and returned to the remains of the cabin. There wasn't much left inside to salvage, so he started a small fire next to the Tower. It was difficult to do with the wet wood, so he used his ripped shirt to get it started. He took the piece of cloth from his pocket and threw that into the fire as well. Then he sat on the plank underneath the Tower's protection and stared into the flames.

The snow began to turn to rain.

"I never thought I would miss home," he admitted to the Tower, his voice quavering as he shivered.

The raindrops pattered above him and he sunk his head in between his knees, wrapping his arms around his legs. His long, matted hair obstructed part of his view. He watched as the snow chipped away with each drop, seeping down into the soil below. Soon the ground would be nothing more than a bloated mess of sludge.

There was something inherently sad about snow, he thought. The symphony of elements that collaborated to blanket the land with its beauty was always in vain. No matter how tightly it clung to every blade of grass or groove of brick, it was always temporary. How quickly the rain washed it away.

The rain reminded him how easy it was to destroy. Destruction didn't need perfect conditions.

The patter of the rain washed his thoughts away too. He sank deeper onto his knees and closed his eyes, sliding back into the world of dreams he hadn't visited in a long time.

It was dinnertime again. Mr. and Mrs. Blue sat adjacent to each other, while Arnold sat across from them. The hum of the television drowned out their chewing and the clanking of their silverware. The nightly newscaster was giving his rhetoric on the current state of the country. No matter the night, there were always problems. Mr. Blue watched intently and scoffed when the newscaster spoke of a politician he loathed, which was most of them.

"How can you not love this guy?" he asked while shoving bread into his mouth. "He's so smart, while all these people running our country are idiots."

There weren't many nights Arnold would reply with anything but a "yeah." It was always easier to agree with Mr. Blue, finish dinner quickly, and retreat upstairs. This way Arnold could avoid any confrontation and they could continue to live civilly.

It was only on rare nights that Arnold felt compelled to speak his mind.

"You know all his opinions are biased, right?" Arnold interjected. "He has to say what the network wants him to."

"No, not true. He actually knows what he's talking about. He's a very smart guy. You know he went to one of the most prestigious schools in the country, right? You don't think he knows what he's talking about?"

"I'm sure he does. I'm just saying, he's biased. That's why you like him. He says nice things about people you like."

"You want your father to start watching your dumb shows instead?" Mrs. Blue asked.

Her sudden hostility jabbed him in the stomach. She had a knack for that.

"That's not what I'm saying. And they're not dumb shows just because you don't like them."

Arnold's appetite began to wane and he slowed his eating to a crawl. Mr. Blue placed his hand on Arnold's arm, a sort of condescending smile on his face.

"Arnold, let me tell you something. He's been on television for twenty years, informing this country and exposing all the lies. It's your generation that doesn't understand. You're surrounded by people who have no idea what they're talking about. When you come to be my age, you'll understand the difference."

"Listen to your father. Learn from him," Mrs. Blue added.

Mr. Blue removed his hand and continued his dinner, unfazed, while Arnold coughed up that conceding "yeah" lodged in his throat, his appetite completely lost.

Most nights played out the same way. Arnold's view on things never seemed to matter to them. They rejected the ideas he proposed for reasons he could never understand. There was so little they ever saw eye to eye on.

Politics.

School.

Arnold himself.

But one day he would make them see his point of view. He'd make it very clear.

Arnold opened his eyes to find the fire burning low. The rain had slowed to a drizzle. He stepped out into the muck and watched it part under the weight of his boot. He picked through the Tower, looking for something to use as a gravestone for Annie, and found a small ironing board. It was the best option, he figured, given its shape and length.

He made his way back to where he'd last seen Frederick, but he was nowhere to be found. Arnold scanned the ground, looking for footprints, and spotted a trail leading back into the forest. He kicked up the brake of the Tower and headed in once more.

It was a tough trek. Every few feet Arnold had to scout ahead to make sure there was a clear path for the Tower while also continuing to follow Frederick's trail. The footprints seemed to go on forever. He passed the point he had reached earlier while looking for him and Annie, by the giant red oak trees, and kept going.

Finally the trail seemed to end and the footprints veered off to the side. Arnold parked the Tower next to a tree and grabbed the ironing board and lantern hanging from the broom. The footprints became erratic, with signs indicating that Frederick had fallen down many times. He reached a thick bush and brushed some branches to the side. He saw Frederick on his knees, Annie's body wrapped up in a blanket in front of him. Arnold approached him from behind until Frederick heard him.

"It doesn't matter how far I go!" he exclaimed, his voice cracking, breaking the silence of the forest. "They're just going to keep tearing the forest out of the ground, aren't they? Eventually they'll tear her out of the ground too."

Arnold stopped, keeping a distance between them. He placed the lantern on the ground, the board still in his hands. The soft glow of the lantern created a dome of light around them.

"It's not your fault," Arnold said, trying to comfort him.

"It is," Frederick replied as his voice began to tremble. "I knew . . . I knew for weeks. . . . I knew for weeks they were coming . . . saw the signs . . . saw the machines lining up, getting closer each day. I thought I could stop them. I thought they would listen, and know, that all the times I spoke out, all the times I protested . . . I was just so lonely. I thought they'd leave it all alone, but I was wrong. I was wrong about them . . . wrong about myself."

He paused to wipe his eyes.

"And for what? What was it all really for? Her? She didn't deserve this." He started crying again. "She was all I had left."

Arnold stood in silence, his head down.

"I'm sorry, Frederick," he finally said. "I know what it's like to lose something you care about. It's a terrible feeling. But you're not responsible for what happens after this."

There was a moment of silence between them. Frederick stood up, his head still down.

"I'm sure that's real easy for you to say, Arnold," he said, looking up now. "Is that what you'll tell yourself when you leave me? That you're not responsible for what happens when you're gone?"

"Frederick, that's not—"

He turned to face Arnold. "I don't want to hear your excuses! You were supposed to help me stop those machines. Why didn't you?"

"I did what I could, Frederick," Arnold said as he placed his hand in his pocket, worried that the piece of his shirt might somehow still be there. "I guess it wasn't enough."

"You know, ever since you've arrived, it's only been about you. You never really cared about this," Frederick said. "If you weren't so selfish, she might still be alive. So don't pretend like you care now."

Frederick was right. In the last week and a half they'd been together, Arnold realized, all he'd been talking about, all he'd been thinking about, was the Tower, and Kingdom. He hadn't even noticed, but they'd become the only things he was interested in, and he'd done nothing to hide this fact.

"Frederick . . . I—"

"Save it," Frederick sneered as he kneeled down again and picked up Annie's body. "You don't have to pretend anymore."

He walked past Arnold, giving his shoulder a shove, and continued into the forest.

"Why couldn't you make your *own* life?" Arnold yelled out to Frederick. "It didn't have to be this way!"

Arnold was riddled with guilt. For a third time, he wanted to call out to someone and tell them he would stop his journey to join them. First it was Charlotte and her friends, then it was Ilium, and now it was Frederick.

He didn't want to abandon him. But he had already abandoned his journey before, and that was no longer an option. Stopping now would undermine everything he had accomplished, including coming back from the dead in the underground village. Leaving home, punishing his parents, stealing the things his family valued . . . Leaving now would render all of that useless.

He wanted to tell Frederick that he would stay. But despite how easy it would be to give up again, he knew he had to leave. He knew he had to go on. As hard as it was, as bad as he felt, Kingdom was calling for him. It had become so much bigger than just him, or the Tower. He had a responsibility to himself. His journey couldn't be for nothing.

When Ilium told Arnold that he needed to be fixed, he thought having the Tower by his side again meant he had achieved that, but now he thought otherwise.

Maybe he was wrong to let me leave, Arnold thought.

He walked a few steps toward where Frederick had gone, but he couldn't see him anymore. It was the last time Arnold ever saw Frederick. It was the last time he ever saw Annie, too.

He walked over to the Tower, the ironing board in his arms, and shoved the board into the soil. Some mud flew out and smacked him in the face. He rocked the board back and forth until it was buried about halfway, resembling some form of a gravestone to anyone who might pass by. He kneeled down beside it.

He wasn't sure what he wanted it to mean. He wasn't sure what had actually died in the forest, but he wanted to believe he'd planted the gravestone for Annie.

The Tower watched him and made Arnold feel like he was being judged.

Whether the gravestone would remain intact for years or be dug up in a day didn't matter anymore. Whether it was right or wrong to leave Frederick to wander alone didn't matter anymore. For better or worse, this was Arnold's life now. This was his path.

He kicked in the brake and pushed the Tower through the mud, heading east again. And for the first time on his journey, the Tower seemed to push back.

A few nights after the metal city could no longer be seen on the horizon, Arnold had a dream. It was one he had dreamed many times since the beginning of his journey.

He was back in the snowy forest. The light dusting of snow had risen nearly three feet, and he was pushing the Tower through it. He wasn't sure where he was going, but pushing the Tower took all his might.

As he marched through, a figure appeared in front of him, a woman with no face. She wore a red silk robe that draped past her knees and loosely hung over her shoulders, unfastened at the waist. Before he could say anything, the woman was on him, holding Arnold down in the snow with her knee on his throat. The powdery snow smacked his face as he tried to wrestle the woman off his neck, but his attempts were futile. No matter how hard he pushed and squirmed, the woman overpowered him.

Then, behind the woman, his father appeared, standing, watching the faceless woman choke the life out of him. And behind his father, Arnold's mother was there, crying. She, too, could only look on in anguish.

Arnold felt as if he were going to take his last breath when, suddenly, he found himself on the shores of a sandy beach, the waves washing in and out underneath him.

He propped himself up onto his arms and looked around. Pieces of the Tower were strewn all over the sand. The tattered remains of the plank and twisted metal of the cart stuck halfway into the sand. A crab scuttled by and grabbed the wooden board with the word *Libri* on it in its claw while flocks of seagulls pecked at the Tower's remains.

Then the tide rushed in, each surge reaching farther and farther up the shore. Arnold was unable to move as it reached his mouth, drowning him. He gasped for air and woke up with a startled cough.

Arnold tried to remember where he was as the first few seconds of being awake carried remnants of the dream. He shook his head and rubbed his eyes. He had to remind himself it was just a dream.

His name was Max. Apart from that, there wasn't a lot Arnold knew about him. Arnold was too young to remember much about Max when he was alive. But he knew Max used to fit in the palm of his hand. He knew Max loved to play in the snow.

The day Arnold fell in love with Max was the day they took Max away from him.

He remembered the day well. It was midafternoon on a Saturday, and Arnold was sitting on the kitchen floor, petting Max's rough, bloated body through the grate of his steel cage. Max was leaning up against the grate, his excess skin poking through every hole. He sluggishly wagged his tail.

Mr. Blue came downstairs and walked into the kitchen. He put his arm through one sleeve of his jacket and then stopped short. He didn't expect Arnold to be there. Mrs. Blue stood at the top of the stairs in a damp robe, a towel wrapped around her head. Mr. Blue walked over to the cage and let Max out. The steel creaked how Arnold imagined a door to a prison cell would.

"What're you doing?" Arnold asked.

"I'm taking him," said Mr. Blue, unable to look Arnold in the eye.

Almost on cue, Mrs. Blue called out. "Arnold, can you come upstairs please?"

He followed her voice to the top of the stairs, but upon arrival it was clear she had nothing prepared. She told him to go to clean his room, but Arnold was notorious for keeping it tidy.

The ignition of an engine outside made his heart jump and sent a rush of nerves through him.

He ran back down the stairs, vaulting over the last three steps. His mother called for him to stop and stay inside, but he didn't hear her.

Arnold burst through the front door. The white-hot sun blinded him. Their Ford Windstar pulled out of the driveway and began turning down the street. He sprinted toward it, letting out a desperate scream for his father to stop. The van screeched to a halt, and Arnold caught up to it, his heart racing.

Through the backseat window, Arnold watched Max pace nervously. Mr. Blue lowered the window for their final moments. In a swell of anxiety, Max desperately tried to jump out the window, but he was too big. Arnold reached in and pet his face, scratching the top of his head and behind his ears. Arnold didn't fully know what was going to happen, but it seemed Max's instinct told him what was to come.

He whimpered while Arnold scratched behind his ears and Max licked his arm. His father exclaimed that he had to go and suddenly pulled away and sped down the street, blowing past a stop sign and nearly hitting another car.

Arnold stood there in the middle of the street, in the wake of the van's tracks. The sun beat down on his sweaty back. In the neighbors' yard, Mr. Wu's kids were throwing a Frisbee around. Ten years later, Arnold would leave town and forget they ever existed. Ten years later, he would still remember Max and all the things he never knew about him.

9

THE OMEN

Pushing the Tower had become a chore. Arnold refused to admit it to himself, but he wore it on his face. The Tower began to consume him as he was forced to rely on it more to survive the long journey east to Kingdom. The holes and depressions that had manifested themselves in the Tower had manifested in him as well.

It was becoming hollow.

He was becoming hollow.

A trail of crushed plastics and stale crumbs traced his path. For months he had been taking away small pieces from the Tower to survive. They were starting to add up.

After so many days of pushing the cart, Arnold could no longer exert the energy necessary to move at a suitable pace. He took half a dozen of his father's belts and knotted them together at each end, fashioning a harness. He fastened them to the far side of the cart and tied the other end to his own belt to pull the Tower behind him.

Without Arnold at the helm, the Tower shook more than usual and the wheels started creaking again. The holes in the Tower created an imbalance in its movement that he had to correct by leaning slightly to the left. All of Moon's renovations were beginning to deteriorate.

Recently he'd endured a torrent of rain that had lasted almost an entire week. Day after day brought a steady downpour that soaked the lands, and even when it subsided for a bit, he was met with heavy winds that slashed at the Tower's tarp, carving holes into it. The Tower began to swell from the never-ending rains. Arnold was forced to throw away many things that would not recover: piles of documents, books, and delicate clothing. He didn't need them in the end, but part of him wished they could stay. Now the tarp hung from the perch and flapped in the wind. Stiff and crusty, it smacked the Tower with every bump in the road.

In the days since the weather had cleared, Arnold had noticed a change in the landscape. Dark skies cast a gloomy hue onto the land during the day. Leaves fell from their branches and became brittle on the ground. Grass hardened and turned yellow, and he kicked up dead blades with each step. There was a noticeable quiet blanketing everything, as if every creature except him had followed their instinct to flee. Arnold had become a lone silhouette in a land with no one in it. It was just him and the Tower now, making a journey of incredible loneliness he could have never imagined.

The hard truth, Arnold realized, was the effect time was having on everything he relied on. And there was nothing he could do.

He stopped to rest in a field of dead grass as the air became acrid with heat and humidity. An invisible smoke seemed to hover over him, and it was hard to breathe. Even as he sat on the plank to catch his breath, there was no escaping it. Everything tasted off, like he had eaten something foul and it now coated his tongue in a thick mucus.

He looked at the horizon toward the south and saw a pack of shadows approaching him. It looked like a march, like some sort of pilgrimage. It was the first life other than himself he could remember seeing since the rains had started.

He waved to the caravan as it got closer, not out of kindness but because the sight of other people gave him momentary relief from the desperate feeling in the pit of his stomach. A figure waved back at him, putting him at ease. Life in a place he thought only he existed in.

"Hello!" the figure called to him.

As the caravan got closer, he could see it more clearly: rows of wagons tethered together by thick rope, roofs made of taupe cloth on wooden frames. People were inside the wagons. Men walked adjacent to women and children, pulling the wagons with more ropes. Arnold counted six wagons and probably two dozen travelers.

The figure called out again, this time closer to him. It was an older gentleman with a gray beard and a flat-rim hat. He looked as if he hadn't showered in days. All of them did.

"You lost, stranger?"

"No. Just stopping to catch my breath."

The bearded man looked up at the Tower, then behind it. "Headin' east?"

"Yeah."

"Better hope you get where you're goin' soon."

"Why's that?"

"There's an omen."

An ominous whisper broke out from the group. The bearded man turned and assured them everything was okay.

"Haven't you heard?" he continued. "It's heading north, blanketing the whole country, consuming everything in its path 'n' whatnot."

"What do you mean an . . ."

The people of the caravan went quiet.

"Omen?" Arnold whispered.

"We don't know when it started, or where, really. All we know is that it pushed us out, forcing us to leave home and head north to outrun it. We barely got out with what we've got now."

The bearded man paused, as if pulling together a line in his head.

"I know how this sounds, but it's got everyone spooked. People are fleein' their homes like it's the end of the world or somethin'."

"Have you seen it?"

"No, I haven't seen it, but I've heard plenty of it. And I'll tell you, I believe it enough not to stay put and hope it's all a bunch o' nothin'."

Arnold's insides began to stir. "You said it's taking over the whole country?"

"Far as I know, yes."

The bearded man waited for Arnold's next question, but Arnold's shoulders slumped and he looked at the ground instead.

"Hey, you can ride with us. We'll tie that thing o' yours up to one of the wagons and pull it, no problem."

Arnold walked over to the Tower and put a hand on it. A drop of sweat fell from his brow.

"C'mon, Dad, we gotta go!" a voice called from one of the wagons. "It's still scorched here. We gotta keep moving."

The bearded man was hesitant. He paused for a moment, then walked over to Arnold.

"You should come with us," he said, placing an arm on Arnold's shoulder. "We haven't seen what's causin' this, but we've seen the destruction of this omen firsthand, and there's no tellin' how far it'll reach. It's better you ride with us to be safe, before it's too late, son. My family will watch over you."

Arnold lifted his shoulder to shrug the man's hand off him.

"It's too late for me."

"Hey, I don't mean to scare you. I'm just tryin' to make sure you understand. I don't want to say this is a matter of life and death . . . but it is, son. Whatever reason you got for bein' out here, it's just not worth it."

There was a moment of silence between the two, then Arnold spoke. His voice was deep and seemed to come from a dark place inside him. There was a defiance in his tone that far exceeded the man's persistence.

"Don't tell me what's worth fighting for."

The bearded man made a move as if to pull Arnold by force but then instead drew his hand away and headed back to the caravan. There was a rustling of cloth and indistinct chatter as the people settled back into their respective wagons. Then one by one they carted past Arnold, each one a divine escape he could not grab hold of. The last one made its way past him, going north, and the caravan began to shrink in the distance. Arnold walked away from the Tower and watched the caravan until it was nothing more than a gleaming speck in the sun's rays peeking through the clouds. Then he sat down in the dirt and watched the sun set, waiting for another caravan to appear, one that would tell him there was no omen, no force seemingly making its way across the land, consuming all in its path. The caravan would tell him there was nothing to fear.

But that caravan never came. The omen was on a warpath headed straight for him. He had reached the point of no return.

Sitting with his legs crossed in the dirt, Arnold finally acknowledged the string of lies he had been telling himself.

"I'm never going home," he admitted.

There would be no family embrace or tearful reunion with a celebration of life once thought lost. He was gone. And so was his family.

The sky turned dark and Arnold still hadn't moved from his spot. The caravan had disappeared hours ago, and once again Arnold was the only life in the scorched land.

In the faint light of the moon behind the clouds, he looked back at the Tower. The word *Libri* stared at him. His eyes were heavy and he felt the veins behind them pulse with every beat of his heart. He bore the image he'd seen painted on his father's face every night, the look of the last remnant of his soul breaking.

He thought about his family and what they might have been thinking at this exact moment. He wanted to believe they were thinking the same thing as he was, that they wished they could take it all back and start over, but truthfully, he didn't know. He'd never know. The regret of putting them through this ordeal was starting to set in. But more than regret, it felt like shame. He wondered where they could be, if they'd recovered at all in the days after his departure. He wondered if he had succeeded in bringing them together or succeeded in further tearing them apart. Only one of the two could be true.

He felt trapped in his own mind and the guilt hovered over every thought he had: guilt for beginning such a ridiculous journey, for changing the course of his family's lives forever. He could barely muster up the feeling from that night, barely feel the flames within his own heart that had made him tear apart his home and rob his parents of everything they owned.

The only heat he felt now was of the air around him, and it was dry and stale, chapping his lips. Everything had betrayed him: his mind, his body, the Tower . . . and now the land itself.

He got up and made his way back to the Tower, its misshapen silhouette standing like some ancient spire. It was alien. It was deteriorating. It was the last hope he could cling to.

The scorched terrain and the rising heat made Arnold thirsty and on a constant search for water. As he wandered through the land, he had to take advantage of any opportunity where water presented itself, and fill the number of plastic bottles he had accumulated from inside the Tower.

One day he came upon a basin that led to a pond, roughly the size of a swimming pool. Cracked mud and dehydrated dirt surrounded the pool of water and in a few days, it would probably evaporate into nothing.

Arnold stopped and parked the Tower just outside the cracked mud, so as not to risk the Tower losing its ground. He unfastened the belt around his waist, untethering himself from the Tower. Hot and sweaty from walking, he got down on his hands and knees and dunked his head in the water. He stayed there for a few seconds and then pulled his head out, wiping his face with his hands and smoothing his hair back. The relief he felt was immeasurable.

Across the pond, Arnold saw something flapping in the wind. An olive blanket, or tarp, seemed to be waving at him. Arnold raised an eyebrow at it. Then he dipped his hands into the water once more and splashed his face before standing up.

He slowly walked along the edge of the pond to get a better look. Once he was close enough and saw it more clearly, he stopped, batting away a swarm of flies around him. It was indeed a blanket. The corner of it flapped in the wind, concealing two large figures and one smaller figure underneath it. Bodies. Arnold stood frozen as a gust of wind passed by and revealed part of one of the bodies. He caught a glimpse of the head that belonged to the smaller body; dark-orange hair that had been braided in pigtails. Closer to the water were three large rucksacks that had been opened. A mess of plastic containers and bottles and opened supplies tumbled along the dirt in the wind. A number of shoes were scattered among the litter too, some of them floating in the pond. Arnold looked at the water, then back at the bodies, and began shaking excess water from his hands and wiping his lips with his forearm.

He swallowed a large lump in his throat and slowly moved away, heading back toward the Tower. He quickly refastened the harness to his belt and kicked the brake up.

He looked over at the bodies once more, and a chill ran through his spine as water dripped onto his shirt. Then he continued walking, pulling the Tower as far away from the pond as possible.

10

IGNORANCE

In the days after the caravan had come and gone, the air had become heavy and hot, and every motion Arnold made felt like he was carving through a thick smog. Even the rare breeze brought no relief. Day and night, he dripped salt water from his brow. The ground beneath him was dry and black, as if wildfire had swept across the land overnight.

Arnold did what he could to endure the heat wave. He secured two brooms that stuck out a few feet from either side of the Tower and then tied several shoelaces between them. There he hung up the clothes that had become too soaked, and let them dry. He rotated his shirts and undergarments, sliding each piece to one side as he hung new ones up.

When the heat became unbearable, he thought about his days in the forest. The crisp, cold air. The cool breeze. The fresh snow. Then he thought about his final day in the forest with Frederick and snapped out of it. The cool winds of the steel city were nothing more than a memory now, and the sapping heat, he decided, was better than the lingering thoughts of sadness.

As the hot days started to wear him down, a southern wind came in, turning into punishing gusts that swirled around him. It scooped up dust and dead grass, creating vortexes that Arnold had to shield his eyes from. He tore an old white T-shirt into strips and wrapped them around his head and mouth, leaving slits open for his eyes. The wind was fierce and angry, as if it wanted to blind him.

Arnold searched the Tower, near where he had first discovered the tarp. There he found a face mask that the builders had worn while they renovated the bathroom in his parents' bedroom. The mask was badly water damaged, smelling of mold. He tossed it to the side, reached into the Tower once more, and pulled out a steel splatter screen. He threw it up into the perch and climbed inside. Here he opened the toolbox and pulled out a pair of scissors. In the perch, he was momentarily safe from the dust.

He cut the mesh screen into a six-inch strip and shoved the scraps into the wall. He unraveled his head wrap and placed the strip over the eyeholes, using the remaining strips of the T-shirt to secure the screen to the head wrap. Then he placed it back onto his face to test it out. The sharp metal poked through the cotton and into his cheeks. It was uncomfortable, but he was willing to trade comfort for sight. With his new head wrap secured, he hopped out of the perch and back into the dust storm.

He endured this for days. His cheeks bled as the steel scraped his skin. The dust never settled. The winds never stopped. The howling storm echoed inside his head and there was no relief.

The omen was real and it was everywhere.

He spent his nights in the perch, where he lay, hungry, restless, contouring his body to the shallow hole, hoping for a few minutes of sleep before half of him became numb and he had to shift again.

"How did this happen?" he asked himself over and over.

When his stomach grumbled at night, he thought back to weekday mornings at home when he was younger, getting ready for school. As he was running late and scrambling to make it to class on time, his mother would have his breakfast waiting for him on the table before he even got downstairs. But like all the other sentimental memories that plagued his mind, she eventually stopped that, too. It was just another thing that had faded away with time. He didn't appreciate it then. He would do anything for it now.

As the days continued to pass, he spent less time traveling and more time seeking shelter in the Tower. His face swelled up from the cuts on his cheeks opening and closing too many times, and he feared they would scar. He feared he would never again look like the person he was when he'd first left home. With his face swollen and bruised, his skin dry, lips cracked and bleeding, he realized how naïve he had been. He wondered how much more naïve he could be.

One night, while he lay in the perch, waiting for the sensation in his body to return, he thought about the last time his entire family had been together. It was his father's fortieth birthday. Family from all over had come to celebrate at a restaurant they had rented out for the night. People he didn't recognize, claiming to be cousins who'd taken care of him when he was in diapers, kissed him on his cheeks, leaving smears of their caked lipstick all over his face. One by one he endured conversations with people whom he shared nothing but a bloodline with. His uncle Pat came to say hello and gave Arnold a high five. He liked Uncle Pat, Mrs. Blue's brother. If ever there was an argument and he was around, he always took Arnold's side. It encouraged him to speak out more than he would have otherwise.

The night came to a head late in the evening, when most of the extended family and friends had already left. Arnold sat at the end of a table, watching his father dance among a group of friends, a group that over the past few years had diminished to just a handful of people. After so many years of canceled get-togethers and broken promises to stay in touch, their friends had grown tired of them.

Arnold began to reminisce about how he and his parents also used to get along, and it suddenly dawned on him how he had been moved to the sideline over the past couple of years. As he looked on, he tried to figure out if his father's smile was because of the alcohol coursing through his veins or if he was genuinely happy to still have those few friends around him. And as Arnold kept watching, he realized it had to be the alcohol. He knew that face well, of putting on a fake smile to hide away from his feelings for just a moment. Arnold knew his father felt sad, because he felt it too.

Arnold was overwhelmed with a debilitating sadness that flooded his eyes, and he broke down, alone at the table as waiters began clearing the plates. Uncle Pat saw him, and he quickly carted Arnold off to the side of the room, near the bathrooms, where he hugged Arnold and let him cry. All the while, his father danced, unaware of his son's anguish.

Arnold never told his parents about that night and neither did Uncle Pat.

Now, as feeling returned to his body, he wondered, had he told his parents how he really felt, of how crushing their alienation had been for him, if the Tower would ever stand as tall as it did now.

The next day, during the few minutes he spent pulling the Tower, Arnold saw something through the dust: a silhouette. He pulled back the screen from his eyes but, in his distraction, lost his footing and fell on his hand and knees. He crawled a few paces, dragging the Tower behind him until finally, and without warning, the storm subsided.

He propped his head up as the dust gave way to breathable air. In disbelief, he tore off his head wrap and took in long, deep breaths. He felt reborn. A massive grin took over his face. It was the first smile he could remember making in a long time. He turned over and fell onto his back and closed his eyes, letting gravity push down on every muscle.

A voice pierced the silence and he turned over to look ahead. A few yards away, on a sloped hill, sat the figure—a girl. Arnold picked himself up and walked toward her. The voice was a little clearer now, but he couldn't tell if the girl was laughing or crying.

Then he saw tears.

The girl seemed like a hallucination to him: long black hair; full, plump nose; thick lips that almost seemed as if they'd been lined with a pencil; a bright yellow dress that may as well have been the sun among the scorched landscape. She sat on a blanket of green grass, while Arnold approached her over the dry brown field.

She sobbed, her face in her hands. Arnold pulled up and sat beside her.

"Are you okay?" he asked, his voice thick and scratchy.

The girl continued to sob while Arnold sat in silence. He wasn't sure what to say and barely had the energy to carry his own head, let alone a conversation. The sudden clarity felt like a haze, and he feared he might be going insane.

Her sobbing tapered off, and her breath hiccupped as she attempted to speak.

"I'm sorry," she said, looking over at Arnold, her hazel eyes red and swollen from what seemed like days of crying.

"That's okay. What's your name?"

"Caroline."

"Hi, Caroline," he replied, unable to look at her. "What are you doing here?"

"I don't know anymore," she replied, seeming to allude to something besides where she was. "What's the point, honestly?"

Arnold dipped his head down between his legs, looking at the blackened earth beneath him. "I'm not sure I'm the right person to ask."

She started sobbing again. "I feel so lost."

Arnold picked his head up and looked around them. Dark smoke plumed from a forest fire on the nearby mountains.

Then Caroline uncurled a piece of paper and handed it to Arnold. He could tell it had been crumpled up many times. A line split the paper in half, with two letters on each side: *L* and *D*. Underneath each letter was a list of words with plus and minus signs next to each one.

"What is this?"

"Never mind. It's stupid," she said as she grabbed the paper from his hand and crumpled it back up. "I'm embarrassed to even talk about it."

"You don't have to tell me if you don't want to, but"— Arnold looked around again at the scorched land—"I'm in no rush."

"It's a list . . . ," Caroline began. "A list of reasons for why I should continue on in this world or give up."

Arnold looked down at the paper in her hands again.

Life. Or Death, he thought.

"Why would you need a list?" he asked.

"Everyone keeps telling me what I should do," she said. "But nobody cares about what I want to do." She threw the crumpled paper onto the ground.

Arnold understood how she felt. All his life he had been told how the world was supposed to be and the role he was supposed to play in it. Like him, she was at a crossroads, trying to decide if she had the strength to take who she was and become what she wanted to be, and if it was even worth it.

"That's not an easy burden to carry," Arnold said. He picked the paper up off the ground. "Can I ask which option has the most going for it?"

She wiped her eyes and pointed to the *D.*

Arnold hunched his head down again and said nothing.

"Aren't you going to try to talk me out of it?" she asked, sniffling.

He shook his head. "You don't need a stranger to tell you if life is worth living or not," he said. "Nobody can convince you but you. And even then, the answer may not be clear. Sometimes . . . you can only go on feeling alone."

She started sobbing again.

Arnold wasn't sure if what he had said was even true. He wondered if it was hopeful to think you could rely on feeling alone, or if it was just a fantasy.

"The head and heart like to fight," he proposed, carefully folding the paper back into her hand. "A lot. And we're never completely sure of the choices we make. But no matter what side you've been leaning toward . . . you need to let the other side win every now and then."

Caroline looked at him and wiped the tears from her eyes, cracking a hopeful smile. Arnold lifted his heavy lips in an attempt to return the smile. She tucked the paper away and flattened out her dress.

"I think you're right," she replied. "I need to think more like you."

She planted a kiss on his cheek and Arnold drew in a sharp breath, startled. She smiled at him again, but he looked away. He took a deep breath in and then looked into Caroline's eyes. His heart started beating faster and his palms began to sweat. She reached over and grabbed the top of his hand and held it there for a moment.

"I think it's time to go home," she said.

"W-wait. What do you mean?" he asked.

"Home."

She gave Arnold's hand a squeeze and then stood up.

"But wait. I . . . I can help you more."

He turned and pointed to the Tower, its fragile silhouette standing out against the bleak background. She glanced at it, un-interested.

"Oh, that's okay. You've given me all the help I need."

She trotted down the hill and out of sight before Arnold could respond. It happened so quickly, he thought she may have been an illusion. If she was, she was the most real anything had felt in a long time.

But what about me? Arnold thought.

He looked out over the hellish landscape to see where she had gone. There was only destruction as far as he could see. He closed his eyes and thought about the day he had fallen into the mountain. That was the day everything had changed. A lingering truth had been exposed that he'd chosen to ignore and bury deep inside. But there was no hiding it now.

This was never his journey to begin with; it was the Tower's.

He stood up and walked toward it, bending down to take off his shoe. He cocked his arm back and threw the shoe at the Tower with all his might.

"You did this!" he screamed at it, his face red and hot.

He dropped to his hands and knees and placed his forehead on the ground. In his heart, he knew his journey to Kingdom was over. Whatever was there for him didn't matter anymore. The omen was everywhere. His only hope was that there was still something to return to. He would have to confront his family, the omen, and every mistake he had made.

He stood up and put a hand on the cart, then kicked back the brake and turned the Tower around.

They were two husks in a dying land.

11

WEST

Away from Kingdom, across the unrecognizable landscape, Arnold and the Tower dug deeper into the earth with every retraced step. For the first time, there was a clear path for him to follow, one he had already walked before. It was safe. It was familiar.

The air was hot and dry. Above him, a flock of birds flew north in a fantastic display of migration. They blanketed the sky and cast a shadow of darkness over him. A fire engulfed the mountains in the distance. There were distorted sounds all around him. He heard echoes of voices and footsteps of creatures he couldn't see.

He searched for a pair of earmuffs to drown out the noise. It was easier to search for things now that the Tower was lighter.

Depressions from where he had previously dug marked Xs on the map of the Tower. He found a pair of earmuffs that used to belong to his mother and tried them on. The white puffs of fur on each end had turned gray from the rain that had punished the Tower. He slid the earmuffs off his head and pulled on one end to widen the headband. It snapped in two immediately, revealing a coating of rust he hadn't noticed.

The sun remained hidden behind the clouds for weeks. The dark color of his skin that had once told the journey of time had all but disappeared. He told himself it would make coping with the end of his journey that much easier. He could safely keep the memories buried forever.

What he had done, where he had gone, who he was trying to become . . . none of it had to be real if he didn't want it to be. He could forget about the whole thing. Arnold knew that reality was hard for him to face, because it meant accepting a life in which every action had a consequence and every consequence meant a changed Arnold.

He stopped at a dried-up lake and parked the Tower near where the shoreline used to be. The cracked ground was peppered with dead fish and birds picking at the rotting flesh. He covered his nose and mouth, trying not to gag from the stench. Swarms of flies circled him, and their incessant buzzing kept him from getting any closer.

He pulled back the Tower a bit and reached into it to pull out a phone that he had unplugged from the kitchen wall. Then he sat down with his legs crossed, looking out onto the dried lake bed in silence. He pulled the receiver up to his ear and waited for a voice to appear on the other end. But it never did.

He flipped the handset over and started typing his home phone number, over and over. The blunt clicking of the keypad comforted him, but the comfort was short-lived.

In the distance, the air was pierced with the howling of some unknown beast. The noise came from the direction he was headed toward. He sat up, leaving the phone on the ground, and kept going.

He looked ahead at a path leading into a cavernous mountain range and knew he had to pass through it to stay on course. The path would lead him back to the home of the scaly creatures, back to Moon and Ilium. The clouds hung low and heavy, ready to burst, but he pressed on anyway.

The weather quickly took a turn for the worse. Just minutes into Arnold's trek up the mountain trail, the clouds exploded over him. Gale-force winds whipped him around like paper, and a torrential downpour punished him, impeding every step he took up the trail. Lightning crashed overhead. Arnold's yellow raincoat whipped viciously while his hood stuck to the back of his neck. Water surged down the trail and he pulled the Tower up closer to him, tightening the loops on the belts tethering him to it. He slipped on every stone in his path and got down on his hands and knees to stay grounded while the Tower rocked from side to side with each gust.

He had to find shelter.

The trail was muddy from the surging waters, and neither he nor the Tower could suffer it much longer. Ahead, the trail split, with one path leading to an overhang and the other rounding out to the edge of the cliff face and down a hill. He climbed his way toward the overhang. He crawled, hand and foot, digging his nails into the muck. One slip off a large rock in his path sent him careening forward, and he landed facefirst in the mud. He spit out the muck and kept crawling.

Finally he was able to drag himself underneath the overhang and he pulled the Tower next to him, out of the storm. The sudden relief sent a shiver through his chest and up his throat. He scraped his palms against the ground to get rid of the mud and wiped it from his face. He peeled off his raincoat and threw it to the side. They sat together, Arnold and the Tower, under the protection of the overhang, soaked to the skin.

A strange sensation came over him. Waves of pressure began forcing their way up his throat. His lips convulsed and he dug his face into his hands, unable to cope with the strange feeling attacking his body. A bubbling whimper escaped his mouth; he could hold it back no longer. He wept loudly and without restraint, his body shaking with every breath he tried to catch. It was a wild sob, one that had been buried for a long time.

The storm died down and his cries echoed, snapping him back into reality. He continued to whimper as his breath caught up to him. He looked around, embarrassed for how fiercely he had cried.

He looked up at the Tower as it gazed out into the valley. He curled his nose and pursed his lips, and with one mighty shove, pushed it away from him, just out of the overhang's reach.

After a few heavy breaths he spoke to the Tower. "Why?" he asked. "Why did you let this happen?"

The Tower did not respond. Arnold looked out into the distance and thought about all the things he and his parents could have done to stop the Tower from ever being born. The possibilities climbed on top of one another in his mind, and then he said the only thing he could muster up.

"I wish I had—"

Suddenly the Tower nudged forward. A rock fell from above the overhang. Arnold looked on, his eyebrows curled. The Tower nudged forward again, this time even farther and toward the edge of the cliff. Arnold scrambled onto his hands and leapt for the cart, falling just out of its reach. He chased after the Tower as it started slipping over the cliff. Arnold grabbed hold of the leather belts tied to his waist and dug his heels into the ground with all his might, letting out a yell that echoed through the valley. The Tower's weight dragged him closer to the edge as it hung half suspended in the air. He let out another yell, willing himself to hold the Tower up.

A voice called out from above.

"Arnold!"

He turned his head to see.

It was Cameron.

"I found you!" he exclaimed in pure delight. "I *knew* I would find you!"

Cameron was older, fiercer, and more frightening than ever. There was a gash on his forehead, the dried blood around it indicating he had been hurt recently. It was clear to Arnold that Cameron had come a long way to find him.

"Cameron?" Arnold called out in disbelief. "What are you doing here?"

He hopped down from the overhang and moved toward Arnold.

"You have no idea what I've gone through, Arnold!" he yelled. "And now you're going to give me back what I deserve."

"What are you talking about?" Arnold called out, his arms shaking from the weight of the Tower.

Cameron held his hands out in front of him and flexed his arms, trying to channel energy into his fingertips.

"Yes, I can feel it again," he went on, his eyes closed. "It's all coming back now."

Arnold ignored Cameron as he wrestled with the leather belts, trying to gain enough leverage to pull the Tower back onto solid ground. Cameron, his eyes still closed, also continued to strain. His arms shook now as he tried with all his might to force out some kind of power. Finally, when nothing happened, he relaxed his muscles and opened his eyes again. He pulled his hands toward his face.

"It's true then," he said. He looked back at Arnold, who had managed to slide half of the cart back onto the ledge.

"I know what I have to do." He squinted at Arnold, his gaze sinister.

He marched toward Arnold and the Tower. Arnold caught him.

"Cameron, stop!"

"Get out of the way, Arnold. This is bigger than you."

"Listen to me! You don't have to do this!" Arnold yelled, desperately trying to pull the rest of the Tower onto solid ground. The wet earth made it hard for him to gain much traction.

"You don't understand—" Cameron said. Suddenly, he grabbed his head, as if a sharp pain had just struck him. He doubled over, wincing.

"Stop!" he shrieked. I don't want to do this." Cameron seemed to be wrestling with his own mind.

Arnold saw that he was distracted, and continued to pull the Tower up, one belt notch at a time.

Cameron fell to one knee, holding himself up with one hand, the other holding his head.

"Why are we doing this—"

"Why am I destroying it—"

"I have to destroy it—"

Cameron spoke to himself, back and forth.

The Tower was almost fully upright now.

On the ground next to Cameron was a rock almost the size of his head. He looked at it, still wincing in pain, and picked it up. He got back to his feet and looked at Arnold, who was unaware that Cameron had stood up.

As if acting against his will, Cameron walked up to the Tower and hurled the rock at it. It knocked over a broom holding up a line with Arnold's dirty clothes on it, and spewed a mess of other things onto the ground: books, ceramic ornaments that shattered on impact, and a cardboard box filled with photographs. The dent in the Tower caused the perch above it to collapse; the toolbox and tarp came tumbling down as well.

Pieces of the Tower were scattered all around.

Cameron stood beside the Tower now and placed his hands on it as Arnold wrestled to keep it upright. He looked Arnold in the eye and started pushing the Tower off the edge of the cliff.

"Cameron . . . don't!" Arnold pleaded, his voice strained, every muscle in his body tightening.

"I have to do this, Arnold. It's the only way."

Cameron dug his heels into the ground and pushed the Tower toward the ledge with a big heave. The Tower slid back over the edge and dragged the slack from the belts with it. Arnold fumbled with the belt buckle securing his tether to the Tower as it rocketed toward the ground. The last of the slack went over the edge and forcefully pulled Arnold with it. He had seconds to react and, with one pull of the belt strap across his waist, released the buckle keeping him bound to the Tower. He rolled to a stop, hanging halfway over the cliff.

The Tower plummeted toward the ground. It tumbled and crashed, split apart by rocks and jagged boulders until nothing was left.

Arnold lay there in disbelief, looking down into the valley. Anger bubbled up inside his chest, a hot, fiery rage. He could feel all the emotions he had experienced when he couldn't stand up for himself and all the regrets he'd buried in the graveyards of his mind bursting out of him all at once.

Cameron was breathing heavily, and let out a laugh of relief, sweat dripping down his face.

He put his arms up in front of him again and looked at his palms. A wind blew by and a gust of air rushed toward him.

"Did I do it?" Cameron asked himself.

Arnold quickly got up to his feet and made a desperate charge for Cameron, tackling him to the ground. He rolled on top of Cameron, furiously swatting at his face. They continued to roll along the edge of the cliff, and Arnold grabbed a fistful of Cameron's hair and yanked. They hung over the edge while Arnold gained a grip around Cameron's neck with both hands, squeezing with every muscle. Cameron clamped his hands over Arnold's, trying to pry him loose. Arnold squeezed harder, staring Cameron in the face, gritting his teeth like sandpaper against stone. Cameron stared back, his face turning blue. He released his hands from Arnold's and jabbed him in the face, forcing Arnold backward. He clenched his eyes at the seething pain. Cameron rolled away from the ledge, coughing and catching his breath.

On his hands and knees now, Arnold grabbed a hammer that was lying on the ground. Cameron saw this, and dove at him. He clasped his hands around Arnold's fist and pried the hammer loose from his fingers, wrestling Arnold away from it. The hammer fell just out of Arnold's reach and he struggled to grab it again. Cameron wrapped his arm around Arnold's neck in an attempt to pull him away, but Arnold was able to reach for the hammer and strike Cameron on the hand. Cameron immediately pulled his hand back, howling in pain, and shoved Arnold away with his feet.

They both stood up, Cameron looking behind him to see he was inches from the edge.

"What are you going to do, Arnold?" Cameron urged him, visibly scared. His hand was shaking, and the back of it was already beginning to bruise.

Arnold stood there, breathing as heavy as he ever had in his life, squeezing the handle of the hammer tightly. He gritted his teeth, holding back a well of tears, and rushed toward Cameron once more. Cameron braced himself. Arnold swung at him, forcing him off the edge, and Cameron slipped, grabbing Arnold's arm as he fell backward. Together they tumbled over the edge of the cliff, bouncing off the giant boulders and jagged rocks. Arnold's world swirled around him in a dizzying mess.

Then everything went dark.

A gentle voice invited Arnold to wake up. He opened his eyes slowly as light flooded the room. A thick comforter hugged his entire body, and he felt groggy. Mrs. Blue sat beside him on his bed, running her fingers through his hair, humming a gentle tune. The curtains swayed in the breeze, picking up tiny pieces of dust that danced and then found their way onto a shelf in his bedroom, stacked with toys and games.

"Hi, baby, are you okay?" she asked him.

He propped himself up onto his elbows and rubbed his eyes.

"Hey," he said, his voice heavy with sleep.

"You were talking in your sleep."

"Was I?"

"Yes. Were you having a nightmare?"

Arnold looked around the room. His bedroom back home. It was exactly the way it was before he had left. He turned and sat up, placing his feet on the carpet. The bright green walls and dangling light in the center of his room filled him with comfort.

"It felt . . . so real," Arnold finally responded.

"I know," Mrs. Blue said. "But it was just a dream."

Arnold continued to look around the room, unsure what to make of everything.

"Why don't you go wash up and come down for breakfast?" She kissed him on the head and rubbed his shoulder before leaving the room.

Arnold got out of bed, walked to the window, and looked outside. It was a bright, warm spring day. Across the street, Mr. Sulvich was watering his lawn while their dog, Jenny, ran back and forth through the water. Next door, Mr. Wu's kids, Fai and Huan, were throwing a Frisbee back and forth. Arnold smiled and let the warm air envelop his skin as it wafted through the screens of his window.

He walked out of his room, stepping carefully into the hall. There were noises coming from the kitchen, chatter and the sizzling of pans. He walked down the steps, skimming his hand against the wall the entire way.

In the kitchen, Mr. Blue sat at the table, eating breakfast while Mrs. Blue was busy at the stove, cooking eggs. The smell of coffee wafted through the house.

"Well, look who's up," Mr. Blue said to Arnold, smiling.

"Hey, Dad," Arnold replied, rubbing the back of his head.

"Heard you had a bit of a scare this morning," Mr. Blue said with a wink. "Anything you want to talk about?"

He sat down across the table from Mr. Blue. An empty plate with a fork and knife had been set up for him already.

"No . . . I'm okay."

"Now, now, remember what we talked about. It's not good to keep things inside like that."

Mrs. Blue returned to the table with a hot pan of eggs and slid them onto Arnold's plate with a spatula.

"You can tell us whatever you're feeling, Arnold," Mrs. Blue added. "Don't be afraid."

Arnold looked down at the eggs, perfectly sunny-side up and staring up at him. He grabbed his fork and knife and was about to pierce his eggs but stopped and placed his utensils back down onto the table.

"I dreamed . . ."

Mr. and Mrs. Blue looked at him intently, like they really wanted to listen to him.

"I dreamed I was far away from home. Like, really far. And I left everything behind because I was so . . . angry. About the things that had happened . . . to me . . . to the family . . . but mostly, I was angry at myself, for not being strong enough to say anything. So I ran away. I wanted to start over. I wanted to go somewhere I could be happy. But . . . it all became a nightmare. No matter where I ended up, the same problems found me, because it was me that needed to change. But it was too late. It all went wrong. I ruined everything."

Mr. Blue took another bite of his breakfast and a sip of his coffee, unfazed by the weight of Arnold's words.

"So what did you learn?" he finally asked.

"Huh?" Arnold asked, looking up from his plate.

Mrs. Blue joined them at the table. "What did you learn, Arnold?"

"I . . . I don't—"

But before he could finish, there was a knock on the door. Mrs. Blue got up from her chair and walked over to the entrance. Arnold peeked around the corner to get a better look. Through the doorway, he could see outside, and noticed that day had become night in an instant.

"Oh, you're home late," he heard his mother say to the stranger.

"Yeah . . . I stayed late to do some studying at the library," the stranger said.

The voice sounded familiar to Arnold. He got up from his chair and walked toward the entrance, where Mrs. Blue was helping the stranger take off his backpack.

"I'm fine. Just let me go upstairs."

He recognized the voice clearly now. His heart started to beat rapidly and his breaths became sporadic. Mrs. Blue stepped aside to let the stranger in and then Arnold saw him.

He was face-to-face with himself.

Arnold stood there in disbelief. "I . . . I don't understand what I'm looking at," he said.

The other Arnold marched past him as if he wasn't there and then stormed up the stairs. Arnold walked to the bottom of the staircase and watched. He recognized everything about him: the outfit he wore, the speed of his steps, the look in his eyes.

He knew exactly what day it was.

Arnold had been lashing out at school recently, his parents unaware. He had gotten into a fight with a bully that day and the principal had sent him home for it. It was still early and nobody else had been home. As he hung up his jacket inside the closet, one of his father's blazers slipped off the hanger and fell. Arnold bent down to pick it up, along with some loose change and a crumpled piece of paper that had fallen out of one of the pockets. He scooped them up and placed everything back inside the jacket—all, except the note. Curious, Arnold unfurled it and began to read.

The paper had a smear of lipstick on it with a note that seemed to have been jotted down quickly. The handwriting was feminine. The words revealed Mr. Blue's darkest secret. All those long nights he said he'd spent at the office and sworn were strictly because of the business, were lies.

Upon reading this, Arnold panicked. He quickly folded the note back into its original place and hung the blazer back onto the hanger. Then he ran out the front door. He ran through his backyard, over the creek, and across to the other side of town.

He ran until he found himself in an unfamiliar neighborhood, where he sat on a bench just outside a park. He tried to make sense of everything in his head. He didn't want to believe it, but he didn't want to go home, either. He waited until it got dark out before returning home, and did his best to pretend he hadn't seen anything. He rushed past his mother, up the stairs, and into his room, closing the door. Inside, he began to create something that would allow him to cope with it all.

The Tower.

Mr. Blue was standing in the kitchen entrance now, staring at Arnold, a look of shame in his eyes. Mrs. Blue looked at him too, her eyes filled with grief.

Arnold looked at them both and then down at the floor.

"I'm sorry," he said. "But I have to go now."

He took a deep breath.

"I have to."

12

EQUILIBRIUM

Half dark. Half light. The silhouette of his nose. The rhythmic creaking of wooden spokes. Blinding sunshine entered the cabin between the hem of the cloth stitching. A blanket of pain and pressure covered his left foot, left knee, left hip, ribs, upper back, head, and right eye.

It was quiet. Then it went dark again.

Half dark. Half light. The silhouette of his nose. The rhythmic creaking of wooden spokes. Still there was pain and pressure.

Arnold sat up. He was shirtless, wrapped in bandages around his torso, left leg, and knuckles. He gently grazed his fingers across the blind side of his face and felt the ridges of more bandages. A searing pain cooked underneath them.

He looked around. From the light through the cloth stitching, he was able to make out the cabin of a moving carriage. Dozens of steel hooks were nailed into the wooden supports, with top hats of all different colors hanging from them. A yellow top hat hung right above him.

He pulled himself over to a corner of the cabin and recounted everything, playing it over and over in his mind. No matter how many times he played the memory back, no matter what he thought, nothing changed.

Now here, inside a moving carriage, he was alone.

He fell asleep again and woke up back on the floor, with fresh bandages. A gray top hat hung above him. His stomach growled with hunger, but the severe pain he felt everywhere else stole the spotlight.

After some time, the carriage came to a stop. Feeling an overwhelming indifference, Arnold didn't budge.

He heard the driver get down from his seat and walk around the side of the carriage, his steps soft. Arnold assumed it was a he. The driver stopped in front of the carriage opening and shuffled around for a few seconds. Then the cloth opened and light flooded the cabin, blinding him. Arnold squinted to get a look at the silhouetted figure.

"Oh, you're awake. My pardon," the voice said, startled. It was warm and rich, like a radio broadcaster's voice. The figure was tall, very tall—the crown of his head almost reaching the top of the carriage's opening.

"Are you feeling much discomfort?" he asked.

Arnold's uncovered eye adjusted to the light, and the figure took form. It was indeed a man, but one unlike any he'd ever seen. The figure was wrapped from head to toe in navy fabric, woven around each limb like a mummy's cloth. Only the top half of his face—eyes and nose—could be seen. His eyes were a deep blue and his face pale white, like a man who had just seen a ghost or had become one himself.

"I won't climb in unless I have your permission, but I would like to check on your wounds," he said. "I don't believe you've broken anything . . . but your injuries are concerning."

Arnold sat there subdued, sulking. The man started nervously tapping his foot and stroking his chin. Arnold lifted his droopy eyes, the covered eyelid brushing against the bandage, and took notice of the man's yellow top hat.

He opened his mouth as if to speak to the man but simply nodded instead. Shame was written on Arnold's face.

The driver climbed in, ducking so as not to hit his head on the ceiling, and kneeled down beside him. A medical kit appeared from somewhere, and the man pulled out a roll of navy bandages. He looked at Arnold anxiously.

"Not to worry," he said. "I assure you these are fresh."

Arnold's face didn't change from his thousand-mile stare.

The driver carefully unwound the bandage from Arnold's eye. The cloth pulled at his skin as the driver gave it a light tug and removed it. The man examined it for a brief moment before unrolling a fresh wrap.

"Can you see?" the driver asked.

Arnold shook his head. The driver began to wrap Arnold's eye with the fresh bandage.

"Would I hate to see the other guy?" the driver asked in an attempt at a joke.

"I don't know," Arnold replied, lips barely moving, his voice raspy.

The driver paused for a few seconds before continuing to wrap Arnold's eye. "My pardon, I don't mean to meddle in your affairs."

"It's okay."

The man finished wrapping and then clipped the end, folding it underneath and then tying it off.

"How is that? Good?"

Arnold nodded.

The driver put away the medical supplies and tucked the kit into a wooden cabinet nearby.

"You must be hungry," the driver said.

Arnold had no reply, though his stomach had something to say about it. The driver looked around, waiting for Arnold to speak.

"Well, I won't assume," he said as he backed out of the carriage. "My pardon, I prefer not to guess what someone wants. That's gotten me into trouble one too many . . ."

He stopped himself, seeming to drift off in thought.

"Well, it will be getting dark soon, so I will be stopping to make food. There are provisions in that cabinet if you prefer to eat alone. I know I like to sometimes."

He fastened the carriage flaps and tied them tight. The cabin went dark again, save for the light seeping in through the stitching. Arnold lay down and stared at the ceiling. The carriage started moving again, and Arnold couldn't help but count the seconds in his head. He stopped counting once he reached for the cabinet.

The next night, the tall man made a fire a few feet away from the carriage. The smoke wafted into the cabin and Arnold stepped outside for the first time. He crossed his arms for warmth.

"My pardon," the man said as he sprang to his feet. His legs were comically long. "I meant to return your garments but did not want to disturb you."

The man, sporting an olive-green top hat, opened up a rucksack next to him and pulled out a white T-shirt. He handed it to Arnold.

"My pardon, I tried as best I could to clean your sweater, but it was beyond my capacity. As you can see, we're quite far from any proper washing facilities, and I do not think you would have wanted to wear it in its current condition."

Arnold took the T-shirt from the man and fumbled it in his hands. It smelled of rusted metal, which produced a foul taste in his mouth. A dull crimson ring surrounded the neckline.

"Do you have another shirt?" Arnold asked.

The man looked at him inquisitively. "My pardon, but I do not. I don't have much use for regular clothing these days."

Arnold begrudgingly put the shirt on. The tall man looked on, a bit disappointed.

"Have you come to join me for supper?"

"I just need some air."

Arnold walked over to the fire and sat outside the ring of light. The tall man sat back down inside the glow of the fire. It was quiet, with only the crackling of wood to break the silence. They sat there for a while, both staring into the flames, in their own separate worlds.

The man nervously played with a stick in his hand. "My pardon, I haven't given you a proper way to speak with me. My name is Gilliam, but most others refer to me as simply Gill."

Arnold looked over and forced a halfhearted smile. "Arnold . . . Blue."

Then there was silence again.

Gill poked at what looked like a bird cooking on a spit. He removed it from the flame and slid it off the skewer, then leaned back and began feasting with his hands.

Arnold finally spoke up. "Why is it so quiet?"

"My pardon, would you like to talk about anything in particular?"

"I mean here." Arnold nudged his chin forward. "What happened to the omen?"

Gill wiped his mouth with his sleeve. "I'm not sure. It seems to have gone away."

"How convenient," Arnold replied as he buried his face in his knees.

"Did the omen do this to you, Arnold?"

The fire danced between them.

"No. I did this to me."

Arnold stared into the light coming from the space between the stitching of the carriage. It was overcast outside and the light was particularly gray. The gentle rocking of the carriage became harsher as the terrain changed. Flat fields turned to hills of stone, with crude paths paved by previous travelers. He had no idea where they were going, but he didn't care. His fate was the same with or without Gill, a future without the Tower, without Kingdom. There was no second-guessing its condition this time. He'd seen it all with his own eyes. There was no creature working to restore it in the night and no dream to wake up from.

The Tower's destruction was absolute.

The carriage sputtered outside and stopped abruptly. Grunts and groans came from the driver's seat. Arnold stepped through the flaps and walked toward the perch. His bandages tightened around his waist with each step. A thin pillar of smoke funneled up from some mechanical contraption in front of Gill's seat.

"Everything okay?"

Gill was visibly frustrated but quickly composed himself upon seeing Arnold.

"My pardon, it's a mechanical issue. I thought the belt cables would last the whole trip, but it appears I've been swindled."

"Are we stuck?"

"Nothing a little tinkering can't fix," Gill tried to assure him, though his words seemed to do little to convince even himself.

That night they camped out near the carriage again. Gill cooked up a rabbit he had caught earlier, and they ate together around a new fire. Arnold finished his portion in silence and leaned up against the large wooden wheel of the carriage. The sky had finally cleared and he stared up at it. Gill wiped his mouth with his sleeve and looked over at Arnold with concern.

"How are you feeling?" Gill asked.

"Been better," Arnold replied.

"My pardon."

There was a moment of silence between them.

"I don't think I've seen the moon in weeks, maybe longer," Arnold admitted.

Gill looked up at the sky as well. "It has been a long time."

"What do you think happened?" Arnold asked of the omen.

"I don't know," Gill said. "But when good things happen, I tend not to question them."

Good things, Arnold thought.

"What do you think?" Gill asked.

Arnold picked up some dirt and rubbed it between his fingers.

"I don't know either."

They went silent again. Gill stood up and stoked the flames of the fire pit with a stick, then threw the stick into the fire. He looked at Arnold, who was still looking up at the sky, then sat back down.

"I can't sleep," Arnold said, unprovoked.

"Why not?"

"I've been asking myself that," Arnold continued. "I lay down and wonder how it's even possible to fall asleep and wake up not remembering when you did. I wake up feeling like I never had any control of it to begin with. Then I wonder, if that's true, how can I trust anything else? Do I have any control at all? Have I just been dreaming?"

Gill pondered it for a moment. "Wouldn't that make me part of that dream too?" he asked.

"I guess so."

Gill let out a laugh but quickly got serious. "Well, if my life has been nothing more than a dream of yours . . . you have a lot to answer for."

Arnold pressed his lips together, afraid to say more. They sat until his eyes became heavy and he climbed back into the carriage to sleep.

The next day, Gill worked to fix the engine while Arnold lay in the carriage. A horrible pain twisted inside his stomach, keeping him awake. He tossed and turned on the floor of the cabin. All he could think about was the Tower. Finally, when it hurt too much to lie down, he emerged from the cabin, catching his breath. He went around the side of the carriage. A mess of tools was scattered on the ground.

He took a few steps away and vomited next to the embers of the fire pit. Gill pulled himself out from underneath the engine.

"Arnold, good morning. Are you okay?"

Arnold hacked up a ball of spit with chunks of regurgitated food in it.

"That's definitely rabbit," Arnold said in disgust.

Gill put his arm around Arnold's shoulders and brought him back to the carriage, where he then helped him to sit down.

"Let me get you some water," Gill said, rushing back to the driver's seat.

Arnold wiped residue from his lips and surveyed the tools on the ground. He spotted a pocket-sized mirror beside a screwdriver and grabbed it, pulling it close to his chest. He looked over at Gill, who was searching through his rucksack, and got to his feet, sprinting in the opposite direction.

"Arnold, where are you going?" Gill called out as he pulled a canteen from the rucksack.

Arnold paid no attention and kept running. He climbed a hill and slid down the other side into a dried-up canal, tumbling and tripping over himself as he reached the bottom. He clutched his side as he sat up, catching his breath. The mirror was a few feet away from him, and he reached over and pulled it closer. The cover depicted a pale woman from the seventeenth century dressed in a fancy gown. The image was faded. He pulled back the copper clasp and lifted the mirror to his face.

A creature with one eye stared back at him. The other eye was swollen and dark from his confrontation with Cameron and the fall they'd suffered. It pulsed with every heartbeat. Just the thought of touching it sent prickles down his spine. He peeled the bandage back and it pulled at his skin. A red-hot pain seared around it, hurting his brain. He let out a painful sigh, dropped the mirror into his lap, and started crying. His unkempt hair swayed in the wind, sticking to his forehead, and the tears somehow found their way out of his deformed eye.

He tried to remember if he had ever cried so much in the past. He had—it was in front of his father.

Arnold and his father were sitting in the driveway after a parent-teacher conference. Arnold was in danger of being expelled for a string of failing grades, and he and his father had been yelling at each other the whole drive home. The yelling was fueled by more than just Arnold's grades. The two of them were always at odds. His father could never get through to Arnold like he wanted to, and Arnold could never explain his feelings to his father.

That night, when they pulled into the driveway, for a moment, something changed.

"I don't want to keep doing this," his father said as he turned the engine off. "It's like every time we talk, it always comes back to the same problem. You have to start looking at the bigger picture, Arnold."

"It's just school. I can fix it," Arnold answered.

"It's not just school. It's everything. This is just the beginning for you. Nothing gets easier, trust me."

"Okay, well, thanks for that."

Arnold looked out his window. It was starting to rain.

"Perception, Arnold. You've got it all wrong, and I don't know how to make you understand."

"What do you mean?"

"You've got this mentality that it's just you out there and that the rest of the world doesn't understand. So you never ask for help or even know when you need it."

Mr. Blue sensed that Arnold didn't want to hear what he had to say.

"How long have you been failing school?"

"I don't know."

"How long?"

"A while."

"Why didn't you ask for help?"

"I don't know."

"If you asked, we would have helped you, either me or your mother."

"No, you wouldn't have, no way," Arnold said, scoffing.

"You don't think we've been to school before? You don't think I've struggled or failed in my life?"

"I'm sure you have."

"Then why don't you ask for help?"

"Because . . ."

"Because what?"

Arnold looked down at his feet. "Because I don't want anybody to try to understand me or figure out my problems. I can do it on my own."

"Why?" his father asked.

"I'm just better alone. It's how it's always been."

"What do you mean alone? What about your friends?"

Arnold's lip began quivering. "What friends, Dad?"

His father placed his hand on the back of Arnold's neck.

"I understand how you feel, Arnold, but you're not alone. And you're not stupid; that's what upsets me the most," he said. "You're smart and you can do great things. I know how you feel. You want to do everything by yourself because you don't think anyone else cares, but it's okay to ask. That's why I'm here. Me, your mother, we're here to help. Everything is going to be just fine."

Arnold couldn't help but cry. He sniffed up a ball of snot in his nose and breathed out in stutters.

"Don't cry. Now you're going to make me cry," Mr. Blue pleaded. "Why are you crying?"

"I don't know."

"I love you, Arnold."

"I love you too, Dad."

His father pulled him in for a hug.

"You're going to be fine. Everything is going to be just fine."

Gill approached Arnold from behind and placed a hand on his shoulder, passing a canteen of water over with his other hand. Arnold stopped himself from crying any more and took a drink.

Gill picked up the mirror in Arnold's lap and placed it in his pocket. "You don't need this right now," he said, and sat down beside him. He picked up a rock and twirled it between his fingers.

The sun started to peek over the clouds in front of them.

"Whatever sadness you feel, you don't have to face it alone," Gill said.

"There's nowhere left to go. Everything's . . . changed."

Gill placed the rock in front of Arnold. "Things change," he said. "But the more important thing is that you change."

Arnold let out a quiet laugh and looked up at the sky. "I was too naïve."

"What do you mean?" asked Gill.

"To think that nothing bad would ever happen, that things would just work out in the end."

Arnold shook his head.

"How could I imagine that everything would just work out? How could I even think that?"

"You're not naïve, Arnold," Gill said. "You're alive. That is the only thing that matters now."

Arnold shook his head a second time. They sat there until the sun moved behind the clouds again and the sky darkened. Gill stood up and wiped the dirt off the back of his pants.

"My pardon, but dinner will not make itself and I've still got an engine to fix. Shall we?"

Arnold nodded, a reflex he seemed to have no control over. He stood up and wiped his pants too, and they made their way back to the carriage together.

"It's getting dark," Arnold pointed out.

"It is," Gill agreed. "Another night by the fire?"

"Sure."

They returned to their broken carriage. Gill continued to tinker with the engine while Arnold boiled a pot of water and pine needles. The quiet night was pierced by the sounds of clanking metal and a crackling fire. Arnold stared into the swirling pot of water as he stirred.

Gill worked through the night and fixed the engine, and when morning came, they continued on. It started to rain and Arnold sat with Gill in the front seat. They were kept dry by an awning above them.

"So where are we going?" Arnold finally asked.

Gill perked up. "I was wondering when you were going to ask me that."

"I'm sorry. I wasn't in the best place for questions earlier."

"I understand," Gill said.

Arnold nodded.

"I would not have taken you much farther anyway. It's not my place to decide your direction. But I am heading north, to my home."

"I see," Arnold replied, facing away from Gill.

"Where are you going, Arnold?"

"I guess north."

"You guess?"

"I don't really know anymore. North . . . east . . . west. They're all the same to me now."

"My pardon, but that sounds like nonsense. North, east, west—those are very different directions."

"I know, I meant . . ." Arnold strained to find the right words.

How can he possibly understand? he thought. *He could never understand my . . .*

Arnold closed his eyes and swallowed the suffocating lump in his throat.

"Gill, if I go west, I'll be returning home, but it may not even exist anymore." He turned to face him now. "And if by some miracle it does, I won't be welcomed with open arms. But if I go back east, there's no way I'll ever make it on my own."

"Make it where?"

There was silence between them.

"It doesn't matter anymore," Arnold said, looking down.

"My pardon, I'm a little confused," Gill said.

"About what?"

"How could your home not want you back?"

"It's complicated."

"What could be less complicated than returning home?"

Arnold lowered his head. "I ruined my home."

He could tell Gill wanted to pry more but didn't have it in him to ask.

"I made a choice. I chose to leave my family and my life behind. I took everything I hated about them and set out to make something better, but I couldn't do it. I failed."

He shook his head.

"Now it's too late. Now it's gone and I have nothing to show for it, nothing worth all the trouble. I should have stopped when I had the chance. I should have stopped when I felt it in my gut. . . . I should have said something."

Arnold picked at some lint on his shirt and flicked it to the side. The wind caught it and it danced in front of him as the carriage moved forward.

"It's okay to have tried and failed, Arnold," Gill said. "Most people don't even make it that far."

Arnold looked at him now.

"And *they* are your family. No matter what you do, no matter how much you have hurt them, destroyed them, they will be happy that you are home. They will always have a place for you."

Arnold looked ahead again as Gill folded his arms and leaned back in his seat, tipping the rim of his hat over his eyes.

The carriage stopped and Arnold stepped down from the front seat. Together, they walked to the cabin and Gill crawled inside. He appeared again shortly, a backpack in hand.

"There's enough here to last you for a while. Rations, fire starters, socks, and, most important, extra bandages. Be sure to change the dressing every few days until your wounds start to dry up. Will you promise me that?"

Gill held out the backpack and Arnold grabbed it. Gill held on tightly to his end. Arnold nodded.

"I promise."

Gill released his grip. Arnold gently swung the pack over his shoulder and pulled an arm through each strap. He and Gill walked back to the driver's seat, where Gill propped himself up, leaning against the carriage. Arnold put a hand on it and looked out ahead.

"Are you sure about this?" Gill asked.

Arnold looked up at him. "I am," he said with a determined voice. "You've helped me all you can, Gill, and I thank you for that. But this is one thing I have to do on my own."

"You're positive?"

"I've never been more sure about anything."

He almost made out a smile behind the navy bandages surrounding Gill's mouth. The carriage sputtered to life, and Arnold backed away as Gill sat up and took hold of the wheel.

"This is your kingdom, Arnold Blue!" Gill yelled over the noise of the engine. "Rule it with conviction!"

Gill tipped his hat in Arnold's direction and began driving. The hum of the engine dissipated as it got farther away. Arnold watched the carriage until it reached the horizon and was nothing more than a tall, shadowy figure. A breeze wisped by. Shivers shot down his spine and the figure vanished.

Arnold was alone now. He rolled his shoulders to adjust the backpack, and looked out north, where the carriage had just disappeared. He placed his hands on his hips and turned to look west, then turned east, gazing into the sun. He closed his eyes. The warmth enveloped his face and he smiled. It was time to begin again.

About the Author

Eric Locsh is a writer and digital marketing copywriter based in New Jersey. He found his inspiration to be a writer from the stories he read as a child and the trips he went on with his family when he was younger. Growing up in a relatively quiet suburban neighborhood afforded Eric the opportunity to create unusual places he could only dream of visiting. *The Tower of Blue* is Eric's first novel.